Dear
Justyce

Dear Justyce

NIC STONE

EMBER

Grateful acknowledgment to Jason Reynolds for use of his work "i am jason reynolds: Day 28 of 30, A Reminder and Reckoning (in need of a rest)." April 28, 2018.
iamjasonreynolds.com/2018/04/28/day-28-of-30-5

Visit us on the Web! GetUnderlined.com

Educators and librarians, for a variety of teaching tools, visit us at
RHTeachersLibrarians.com

The Library of Congress has cataloged the hardcover edition of this work as follows:
Names: Stone, Nic, author.
Title: Dear Justyce / Nic Stone.
Description: First edition. | New York: Crown Books for Young Readers, [2020] | Companion novel to: Dear Martin. | Audience: Ages 14+. | Audience: Grades 10–12. | Summary: Incarcerated teen Quan Banks writes letters to Justyce McCallister, with whom he bonded years before over family issues, about his experiences in the American juvenile justice system.
Identifiers: LCCN 2020020509 (print) | LCCN 2020020510 (ebook) | ISBN 978-1-9848-2966-5 (hardcover) | ISBN 978-1-9848-2967-2 (library binding) | ISBN 978-1-9848-2968-9 (ebook)
Subjects: CYAC: Juvenile detention homes—Fiction. | Family problems—Fiction. | Best friends—Fiction. | Friendship—Fiction. | African Americans—Fiction. | Letters—Fiction.
Classification: LCC PZ7.1.S7546 Dc 2020 (print) | LCC PZ7.1.S7546 (ebook) | DDC [Fic]—dc23

ISBN 978-1-9848-2969-6 (paperback)

Printed in the United States of America
10 9 8 7 6 5 4 3 2 1
First Ember Edition 2022

JUL 27 2022

For Danny Ayers.
You will always be my hero.

Dear Reader,

I didn't *really* intend to write this book.

Sound familiar? It should. It's what I say about writing *Dear Martin*. It's as true now as it was then, though my reasoning's a little different: when I closed the back cover of *that* story, I told myself I was done with Justyce McAllister and the world he inhabited. He'd reached a place of relative peace and come to a deeper understanding of his role as the captain of his own life ship. I felt good, as a book mom, about setting him free to decide where he was headed next and how he'd get there.

But then came the day I received a set of text messages from a pair of boys I'd met *because* of *Dear Martin*—and grown to respect and admire. It went like this (literally):

D: Aye guys.

Z: Whassssuppp

Me: FAVORITES!

D: I've been thinking . . . maybe, just maybe . . . You should make a book about us.

Z: Yessss

D: Like black kids, you know . . . Not like Justyce. Cuz Justyce had hope. He went to a good college.

Me: Tell me more.

D: We don't go to good colleges. We don't

> *have a perfect family like everybody else.*
>
> Z: *That's facts.*
>
> D: *Honestly, we don't even know if we'll live past the age of 18.*
>
> Z: *This stuff me and D go through every day.*
>
> D: *You probably can't put it all in a book . . . but mannnnn.*
>
> Z: *And we got family and friends locked up and everything.*
>
> D: *I know people will listen. You're our voice.*

Since that conversation, I've had the privilege of meeting *many* boys and girls who are very much not like Justyce. Who aren't high-achieving and headed toward blindingly bright futures. Who don't nail their SATs or win debate state championships. I've met them, not at preparatory academies or Ivy League universities, but in "alternative" schools and juvenile detention facilities.

Which made me realize that while Justyce's story might've come to a satisfactory conclusion (for me, at least), there was someone else—a different character—whose story had not: Vernell LaQuan Banks Jr.

If you don't remember him from *Dear Martin* (or haven't read it), don't worry: you will.

He has a story to tell you.

Nic

Even when the condition is critical,
when the livin' is miserable
Your position is pivotal,
I ain't bullshittin' you

—Talib Kweli

PART ONE

The End

Snapshot:

Two Boys on
a Brand-New
Playground
(2010)

It didn't take much for Quan to decide he was leaving this time. He feels a little bit bad, yeah: knowing Dasia and Gabe are still in the house makes his stomach hurt the way it always does when he finds himself faced with grown-people problems he can't fix. But Quan's only nine. Running away *alone* is hard enough. Trying to bring a four-year-old sister and a two-year-old brother just isn't gonna work.

He's glad spring has sprung early. Didn't have time to grab a jacket as he fled. He's pretty sure there was too much commotion for anybody to notice, but he takes a few unnecessary turns en route to his destination in case Olaf—that's what Quan calls his mama's "duck-ass boyfriend" (which is what Quan's *dad* calls the guy)—*did* notice Quan's exit.

What Quan is sure of? He couldn't stay there. Not with dude yelling and throwing things the way he was. Quan knows what comes next, and he couldn't watch again. It was hard enough seeing the aftermath bloom in the funny-looking bluey-purple blotches that made Mama's arms and legs look like someone had tossed water balloons full of paint all over her. He couldn't really do anything anyway. Though Olaf (Dwight is the guy's *actual* name) isn't *too*, too big, he's a whole heck of a lot stronger than Quan. The one

5

time Quan did try to intervene, he wound up with his own funky-colored blotch. Across his lower back from where he hit the dining room table when dude literally threw Quan across the room.

Hiding that bruise from Daddy was nearly impossible. And Quan *had* to hide it because he knew if Daddy found out what really happened when Olaf/Dwight came around . . . well, it wouldn't be good.

So. He made sure Dasia and Gabe were safe in the closet. That was the most he could do.

As Wynwood Heights Park looms up on his left, Quan lifts the hem of his shirt to wipe his face. It's the fourth time he's done it, so there's a wet spot now. He wonders if there will be any dry spots left by the time he gets the tears to stop. Good thing there's no one around to see. He'd never hear the end of it.

He bounces on his toes as his feet touch down on the springy stuff the new playground is built on. There's a sign that says it's ground-up old tires, that the play structures are made from "recycled water bottles and other discarded plastics," and that the entire area is "green," but as Dasia pointed out the last time Mama brought them all here, whoever built the thing didn't know their colors because everything is red, yellow, and blue.

The thought of his sass-mouthed little sister brings fresh tears to Quan's eyes.

He makes a beeline for the rocket ship. It sits off in a

corner separate from everything else, tip pointed at the sky like it could blast off at any moment. Inside the cylindrical base, there are buttons to push and dials to turn and a ladder that leads up to an "observation deck" with a little window. It's Quan's favorite spot in the world—though he'd never admit that to anyone.

When he gets inside, he's so relieved, he collapses against the rounded wall and lets his body slide to the floor like chocolate ice cream down the side of a cone on a hot summer day. His head drops back, and he shuts his eyes and lets the tears flow freely.

But then there's a sound above him. A cough.

The moonlight through the deck window makes the face of the boy staring down at Quan look kinda ghostly. In fact, the longer dude stares without speaking, the more Quan wonders if maybe he *is* a ghost.

"Uhhh . . . hello?"

Dude doesn't reply.

Now Quan is starting to get creeped out. Which makes him mad. This is supposed to be the one place in the world he can *relax*. Where he's not looking over his shoulder or being extra cautious. Where he can close his eyes and count down from ten and imagine shooting into space, far, far away from everything and everyone.

"Yo, why you lookin' at me like that?" Quan spits, each word sharp-tipped and laced with the venom of his rage.

"Oh, umm . . ." The other boy's eyes drop to his hands.

7

He picks at the skin around his thumbs. Something Quan does sometimes that gets him yelled at.

Hmm.

The boy goes on: "I'm sorry. I just . . . I wasn't expecting anybody else to come in here."

"Oh."

The boys are quiet for a minute and then: "I'm Justyce, by the way."

Justyce. Quan's heard that name before . . . "You that smart kid they was talking about on the morning announcements at school? Won some contest or something?"

Justyce again doesn't reply.

"Hellooooo?" Quan says.

"You gonna make fun of me now?"

"Huh?"

Now Justyce looks out the observation window. Quan wonders what he's seeing.

"I wish they would've never made that announcement. Winning an academic bowl isn't 'cool.' Everybody just makes fun of me."

Quan shrugs. "Maybe they just jealous cuz they ain't never won nothin'."

Silence falls over the boys again, but this time, it's not so uncomfortable. In fact, the longer Quan sits there with Justyce above him, the better he feels. Kinda nice not being *totally* alone. Which makes him wonder . . .

"You're a fifth grader, right? You not gonna get in trouble for being out this late?"

"Oh, I will," Justyce says.

It makes Quan laugh.

"I snuck out," Justyce continues. "But it's not the first time, and I'm sure it won't be the last. I think my mama knows I'll always come back."

"Wish *I* didn't have to go back . . ." It slips out, and at first Quan regrets it. But then he realizes his chest is a little looser. This one time at Daddy's house, Quan watched a movie about this big ship that hit an iceberg and sunk, and there was this one scene where the main lady was being tied into this thing that went around her stomach and laced up the back like a sneaker. He later learned it was called a *corset*, but that's what comes into Quan's head when he thinks about his life. "My mom's boyfriend is a asshole," he continues.

The laces loosen a little more.

"He's my little brother and sister's dad, so like I *kinda* get why my mama keeps dealing with him . . ." Little looser. "But I hate him. Every time he come around, he mad about somethin', and he takes it out on my mom."

"Sounds familiar," Justyce says.

"And I be wanting to stick around for my brother and sister but—wait." Quan looks up at Justyce, whose chin is now propped in his hand.

9

All eyes (and ears) on Quan.

"What'd you say?" Quan asks.

"Hmm?"

"Just a second ago."

"Oh. I said that sounds familiar."

"Whatchu mean?"

Justyce sighs. "My dad was in the military and went to Afghanistan. Ever since he came back, he's been . . . different. He drinks a lot and sometimes has these 'episodes,' my mom calls them. Out of nowhere he'll start yelling and throwing stuff." Now Justyce isn't looking at Quan anymore. "He hits her sometimes." Justyce swipes at his eyes.

Quan stands up. "You ever come here during the day?"

"Occasionally." Jus sniffles. "Sorry for crying."

"Man, whatever. Now I see how you won that 'academic' thingy."

"Huh?"

"What kinda fifth grader says *occasionally*?" Quan shakes his head. "I'm gonna head home and check on my brother and sister," he says. "You should go check on your mom."

The boys meet eyes, and understanding passes between them.

"I'll see you around." Quan ducks and slips through the rocket's arched entryway.

He's almost back at the edge of the rubber-floored playground when—

"Hey! Hold up!"

Quan turns around to find Justyce is headed in his direction.

"You didn't tell me your name," Justyce says, out of breath.

Quan smiles—"Vernell LaQuan Banks Jr."—and lifts his hand. "Call me Quan."

"It was real nice to meet you, Quan," Justyce says, smacking his palm against Quan's and then hooking fingers. "Even, uhh . . . despite the circumstances."

Now Quan laughs. "You're ten years old, man. Loosen up."

"Sorry."

"Don't be." Quan shoves his fists in his pockets. It's gotten cooler. "Nice to meet you too, Justyce."

Quan turns on the heel of his well-worn Jordans and heads home.

1

Doomed

Vernell LaQuan Banks Jr. remembers the night everything changed. He'd fallen asleep on the leather sectional in Daddy's living room while watching *Lemony Snicket's A Series of Unfortunate Events* (the movie), and was dreaming about Count Olaf—who'd gotten a tan, it seemed, and looked suspiciously like his mama's "boyfriend," Dwight—falling into a pit of giant yellow snakes like the one from Montgomery Montgomery's reptile room. Screaming bloody murder as he got sucked down into the scaly, slithery quicksand.

Quan's pretty sure he was smiling in his sleep.

But then there was a **BOOM** that startled him so bad, he jolted awake and fell to the floor.

Which wound up being a good thing.

Next thing Quan knew, more police officers than he could count were pouring into the house with guns drawn.

He stayed down. Hidden.

Wouldn't've been able to get up if he tried, he was so scared.

There was a commotion over his head—Daddy's room.

Lots of thumping. Bumping. A yell (Daddy's?). Muffled shouting.

Get down! Put your hands in the air–

Oww, man! Not so tight, you tryna break my arm?

Wham. *BAM!*

Walls shaking.

Was the ceiling gonna fall?

Then the tumult shifted to the left. He heard Daddy's door bang against the wall, then what sounded like eight tons of giant bricks tumbling down the stairs.

Slow down, man! Damn–

Keep your mouth shut!

Quan closed his eyes.

Chill out, man! I'm not resisti–

There was a sharp pain in Quan's shoulder as his arm was suddenly wrenched in a direction he was sure it wasn't supposed to go. A thick arm wrapped around his midsection so tight it squeezed all the air out of him . . . or maybe it all flew out because of the speed at which his body left the ground.

He couldn't even scream. Looking back, *that* was the scariest part. That his voice was gone. That he couldn't cry out. That he'd lost all control of his body and surroundings and couldn't even make a sound to let the world know he wasn't feelin' it.

It's how he feels now as he jolts awake in his cell at the Fulton Regional Youth Detention Center, unable to breathe.

Quan tries to inhale. And can't. It's like that cop's still got him wrapped up and is squeezing too tight. No space for his lungs to expand.

Can't.

Breathe.

The darkness is so thick, he feels like he's drowning in it. Maybe he is. Maybe Quan can't draw breath because the darkness has solidified. Turned viscous, dense and sticky and heavy. That would also explain why he can't lift his arms or swing his legs over the edge of this cotton-lined cardboard excuse for a "bed" that makes his neck and back hurt night after night.

What Quan wouldn't give to be back in his queen-sized, memory foam, personal cloud with crazy soft flannel sheets in his bedroom at Daddy's house. If he's going to die in a bed—because he's certainly about to die—he wishes it could be *that* bed instead of this one.

He shuts his eyes and more pieces of that night fly at him:
Daddy yelling

Don't hurt my son!

before being shoved out the front door.

The sound of glass breaking as the unfinished cup of ginger ale Quan left on the counter toppled to the floor. His foot hit it as the officer with his dumb, muscly arm crushing Quan's rib cage carried Quan through the kitchen like Quan was some kind of doll baby.

The sudden freezing air as Quan was whisked outside in

15

his thin Iron Man pajamas with no shoes or jacket . . . and the subsequent strange warmth running down Quan's legs when he saw Just. How. Many.

Police cars.

There were.

Outside.

Barking dogs, straining against leashes. A helicopter circling overhead, its spotlight held steady on the team of men dragging Daddy toward the group of cop vehicles parked haphazardly and blocking the street.

Quan had counted six when his eyes landed on the van no less than *five* officers were wrestling his dad into.

Wrestling because Daddy kept trying to look back over his shoulder to see what was happening with Quan. He was shouting.

It's gonna be okay, Junior!

Get in the goddam van!

It'll all be fi–

One of the officers brought an elbow down on the back of Daddy's head. Quan watched as Daddy's whole body went limp.

That's when Quan started

Screaming.

Two of the officers climbed into the back of the van and dragged Daddy's body inside the way Quan had seen Daddy drag the giant bags of sand he'd bought for the sandbox he built in the backyard when Quan was younger.

Kicking.

Cut it out, kid!

Wait . . . are you *wet*?

They rolled Daddy to his back, and one of the officers knelt beside him and put two fingers up under his jaw. He nodded at the other officer, who then hopped down from the back of the van and shut the doors.

Flailing.

Screaming.

Kicking.

The taillights of the van glowed red and Quan wished everything would *STOP.* He was sobbing and twisting, and the officer holding him squeezed tighter and locked Quan's arms down.

As the van pulled off, Quan screamed so loud, he was sure his mama would hear him back home some twenty miles away. She would hear him and she would come and she would stop the van and she would get Daddy out and she would get Quan. All the blue-suited Dad-stealing monsters and blue-lit cars would *POOF!* disappear and everything would go back to normal.

Better yet, Mama would bring Dwight-the-black-Olaf, and she'd toss *him* in the back of the van in Daddy's place. And they'd lock *him* up in a snake-filled cell and throw away the key.

Quan screamed until all the scream was outta him. Then he inhaled. And he screamed some more.

17

His own voice was all he could hear until—

"Hey! You put that young man *down*! Have you lost your ever-lovin' mind?!"

Then the officer holding him was saying

Ow! Hey!

And

Hey! Stop that!

And

Ma'am, you are assaulting a police officer–

"I said put him *DOWN*. Right now!"

Ma'am, I can't–

All right! All right!

The grip on Quan's body loosened. His feet touched down on the porch floor just as a wrinkled hand wrapped around his biceps and a thin arm wrapped around his lower back, a sheet of paper in hand. "You come on here with me, Junior," a familiar voice said.

Ma'am, he can't go with you. Until further notice, he's a ward of the state–

"Like hell he is! You can call his mama to come get him, but until she arrives, he'll be staying at *my* house." The woman shoved the paper into the officer's face. "You see this? This is a *legally binding* document. Read it aloud."

Ma'am–

"I said read it aloud!"

Okay, okay!

18

(The officer cut his eyes at Quan before beginning. Then sighed.)

"In the event of the arrest of Vernell LaQuan Banks Sr., Mrs. Edna Pavlostathis is named temporary guardian of Vernell LaQuan Banks Jr. until . . ."

But that was all Quan needed to hear. (Did Daddy *know* he would be snatched away from his son in the dead of night?)

"Come on, honey," she said, and as she ushered Quan away from the tornado of blue—lights, cars, uniforms, eyes—that'd ripped through everything he knew as normal, everything clicked into place.

Mrs. Pavlostathis. The fireball old lady who lived next door to Daddy.

"Let's head inside and I'll go over to your dad's to grab you some fresh clothes so you can get cleaned up. How dare those so-called *officers* treat you that way. The *nerve* of those whites—"

She trailed off. Or at least Quan thinks she did. He can't remember her saying anything else. He *does* remember thinking that under different circumstances, that last statement would've made him smile. He'd known Mrs. Pavlostathis since he was seven years old—she was close to eighty and used to babysit him when Daddy had to make "emergency runs" on weekends Quan was there. Despite her skin tone, Mrs. P let everyone know she was *Greek*, not white.

She was also one of Daddy's clients (*"A little ganja's good for my glaucoma, Junior"*) and, Quan had noticed over the years, the only neighbor who didn't look at him funny—or avoid looking at all—when Quan would play outside or when he and Daddy would drive through the neighborhood in Daddy's BMW.

It was something Mama always grumbled about when she'd drive the forty minutes out into the burbs to drop Quan off. *I don't know why your daddy wants to live way out here with all these white folks. They're gonna call the cops on his ass one day, and it'll be over . . .*

As he and Mrs. P made their way over to her house, Quan wondered if Mama's prediction was coming true.

And in that moment: he hated his mama.

For saying that. Wishing the worst on Daddy.

For staying with duck-ass Dwight.

Putting up with his antics.

For working so much.

For not being there.

Especially right then.

"I'll run ya a salt bath," Mrs. P said as they stepped into her house, and fragrant warmth wrapped around him like a hug from a fluffy incense stick with arms. "I know you're not a little kid anymore, but it'll do ya some good. I just made some dolmas, and there's some of those olives you like, the ones with the creamy feta inside, in the fridge. Put something in your belly. I'm sure you're starving."

In truth, food was the furthest thing from Quan's mind . . . but one didn't say *no* to Mrs. P. So he did as he was told. He stuffed himself with Mrs. P's world-famous (if you let her tell it) dolmas—a blend of creamy lemon-ish rice and ground lamb rolled up into a grape leaf. He ate his weight in giant feta-filled olives.

And when the salt bath was ready, he stripped down and climbed into the fancy claw-foot tub in Mrs. P's guest bathroom.

Quan closed his eyes.

Swirling police lights and Daddy's collapsing body flashed behind them.

Van doors shutting.

Taillights disappearing.

Would Daddy go to prison?

For how long?

What would happen now?

Quan wasn't sure he wanted to find out.

So he sank.

It was easy at first, holding his breath and letting the water envelop him completely. Even felt nice.

But then his lungs started to burn. Images of Dasia and Gabe popped into his head. He remembered telling Gabe he'd teach him how to play Uno when he got back from Daddy's house this time. Little dude was four now and ready to learn.

Quan's head swam.

Dasia would be waiting for Quan to polish her toenails purple. That was the prize he'd promised her if she aced her spelling test. And she did.

His chest felt on the verge of bursting, and everything in his head was turning white.

And Mama . . .

Dwight—

Air came out of Quan's nose with so much force, he'd swear it shot him up out of the water. As his senses returned to normal, he heard water hit tile and the bathroom at Mrs. P's house swam back into focus.

He took a breath.

Well, more like a breath took him. He gasped as air flooded his lungs, shoving him back from the brink of No Return.

It's the same type of breath that's overtaking him now.

Here.

In his cell.

And as oxygen—a little stale from the cinder block walls and laced with the tang of iron—surges down his throat and kicks the invisible weight off him, Quan knows:

He won't die now just like he didn't die then.

He can breathe.

January 12

Dear Justyce,

   Look, I'm not even gonna lie: this shit is weird. I don't write letters to my mama, but I'm writing one to you?
   Smh.
   (Wait, can I even write that? This ain't a text message . . .)
   (See? Weird.)
   (You better not tell nobody I wrote this.)
   Anyway, I had this dream last night and when I woke up, the first thing I saw was that notebook you gave me with all the Martin Luther King letters in it.
   Sidenote: I really do appreciate you popping by to see ya boy before you headed back to that fancy college you go to. Ol' smarty pants ass. But for real, it was good to see you. It, uhh . . . did a lot for me. Gets more than a little lonely in here, and I don't get many visitors, so you coming through was—well, that was real nice of you, dawg.
   Now back to this notebook you left. At first I thought it was wack ("THOSE" black guys, huh?), but the more I read, the more interested I got. Like it was a lot of shit in there about Manny—my own cousin!—that I didn't know because I ain't really KNOW him, know him. That was kinda wild.

23

And YOU! Man, we got way more in common than I woulda thought.

It was one letter in the notebook that made me wanna write this one to you. Not sure what happened (you mentioned doing the "wrong thing"), but there's a line you wrote: "Those assholes can't seem to care about being offensive, so why should I give a damn about being agreeable?"

I don't know what it is, but that shit really got me.

I've never told anybody about the night my dad got arrested. It was a couple years after you and me met in the rocket ship. I was eleven. Cops busted up in the house in the dead of night like they owned the place and just . . . took him.

And I haven't seen him since. They gave him 25 years in prison.

It's only one other time in my life I ever been that scared, J. It all happened too fast for me to figure out what I could do. I think deep down, I knew he was prolly going away for a long-ass time—I was fully aware of his "occupation," and while I was sure the cops wouldn't find any contraband in his actual house (he was real careful about that), he dealt in more than just green, and the net was wide, so it was only a matter of time.

I really miss him, though.

I dream about the whole scenario a lot. Did last night, in fact. And when I woke up and looked at the date? Today is the sixth anniversary.

Shit hit me harder than it usually does. Probably because it also means I've been up in here for almost sixteen months. It's the longest stretch I've ever done, and I don't even have a trial date yet. I do my best to just cruise—not really think about where I am and what it's actually like to be here. But today I couldn't help but notice how bad the food is. How heavy the giant iron doors are, and how . . . defeated, I guess, everyone up in here seems, even though a few of the others talk a good game about getting out.

I keep thinking, like: What would my dad say if he could see me now? How disappointed would he be?

Yeah, what he did for a living wasn't exactly "statutory," as he used to say. But if there's one thing he was hell-bent on, it was me NOT ending up like him. We talking about a dude who used to drop my ass at the library when he had to make some of his runs. (Head librarian had real bad anxiety and was one of Dad's clients so she took good care of me.) Don't nobody know this, but I used to eat up the Lemony Snicket "Unfortunate Events" joints like they were Skittles. You ever read those? Them shits go hard. Kinda wish I had my collection here.

Anyway, that was all him. Vernell LaQuan Banks Sr. He's the reason they tested me for Accelerated Learners and I wound up in that Challenge Math class with you.

He wanted me to do good. To go far and be better.

But then he was just . . . gone.

25

(Sorry for getting sentimental, but like I said before: you better not tell nobody I wrote all this. Or that I used to read books about little rich white kids.)

That night he got arrested turned everything upside down. I knew things were about to get bad because my dad had been like the duct tape holding our raggedy shit together. He paid for a lot and gave my mom money, and he really was the reason I stayed out of trouble. The minute that van drove away with him in it, I felt . . . doomed.

It's why I stopped talking to you. Everybody else too, but especially you. I woulda never admitted this (honestly don't know why I'm admitting it now . . .), but I kinda looked up to you. Yeah, you were only a year older and you were dorky as hell, but you had your shit together in a way I wanted mine to be.

I knew if I could just be like you, my dad would be proud of me.

Seeing what you wrote in that post-whatever-the-hell-set-you-off letter . . . I dunno, man. If YOU felt that way, maybe everything my dad tried to push me toward really was pointless.

Don't really matter now anyway. I'm prolly gettin' WAY more time than my dad did.

Guess it's whatever.

I don't even know if Imma send this. Maybe I should. You better write back, though. Cuz otherwise I ain't never writing you another letter again.

Got me over here pouring my heart out and shit.

Smh.

(There I go again!)

Later,

~~Vernell LaQuan Banks Jr.~~ QUAN

P.S.: I know you already knew my government name, but don't ever call me by it.

P.S.S. (or is it P.P.S.? Yo, you ever heard that song "O.P.P."? I love that song.): REMINDER—don't tell NOBODY I wrote this!

2

Downhill

It's not like Quan didn't *try* to keep it together at first. He really did.

Yeah, he kinda withdrew into himself a little bit. Didn't talk or interact with people as much. But that's because he was trying to stay focused.

It was the only way he knew how to cope: control what he could, ignore what he couldn't. So for a while, he did his homework. Kept his and Gabe's room straight—even though sharing space with a little kid meant cleaning every single day. Played Connect 4 with Dasia. Took both of them to the playground as often as possible. And even there, he was working: keeping the rocket ship cleaned out. He knew some of the stuff he found inside it suggested some not-so-playground-appropriate activities, but he did his best to make sure at least *that* part of the play area stayed kid-friendly.

Weekends he was supposed to be at Daddy's, he spent with his nose buried in books. No matter what else he

28

strayed to, he always returned to *A Series of Unfortunate Events*. Something about watching those kids escape by the skin of their teeth over and over again helped Quan keep his head above water even when everything around him seemed to be crashing down.

Because everything did.

Seem to be crashing down.

Crashing and tumbling downhill like good ol' Jack and Jill.

Shortly after Daddy's arrest, Dwight moved in. Which Quan figured would happen eventually: the only reason he wasn't living with them already was because Daddy told Mama he'd stop giving her money if she

let that piece of shit occupy the same space as

my son.

With Daddy gone, though, money was getting tight. And *Olaf*-ass Dwight used that to his advantage. Told Mama he'd help with the bills—

But I can only do that if I don't have

my own rent to pay.

(Quan overheard the whole conversation. When it was over, he climbed down from his hiding place up on the high shelf in the coat closet where Mama kept the extra bed comforters and went straight to his rocket ship, kicking the hypodermic needle he found inside it right out the entrance even though he knew a little kid might find it.)

(He used a discarded Takis bag to pick it up and put it in the trash can later.)

Even at twelve, it didn't escape Quan's notice that the men in his mama's life—Daddy included—used money to get her to do what they wanted her to. It bothered him no end. But he wasn't sure what he could do about it.

Which became a running theme: not knowing what he could do about anything.

So he stayed focused.

Nights Dwight would come "home" smashed out of his mind—and smashing things as a result—Quan would stay focused.

Mornings Quan would wake up and find Mama's bedroom door locked, but a note from her asking him to get Dasia and Gabe "clothed and fed and on the bus" because she wasn't "feeling too hot," Quan stayed focused.

When the light would hit Mama's face just right and he'd see the bruises beneath her caked-on makeup, Quan stayed focused.

And it paid off. Mama might've been a mess, but Dasia and Gabe were just fine. Despite their daddy being a human garbage disposal, they laughed and smiled and were doing good in school . . .

All because Quan stayed focused.

Quan was also kicking academic ass and taking names. Because despite Daddy's absence, Quan was determined (maybe now even *more* determined) to make the old man proud. Become the upstanding dude Daddy wanted him to be. Quan even considered going out for football once he hit ninth grade.

Daddy had played in high school and even been offered a scholarship to college, but then Mama got pregnant and Vernell Sr. decided to stick around, take care of the son he'd helped create. *Unlike my dad did*, he told Quan once. What better way to pay Daddy back than to achieve the dream Daddy didn't get to live—because of Quan?

So Quan stayed focused.

Then there was The Math Test.

It'd been a little over a year since Dad's arrest. Quan was the only seventh grader in the Algebra I Challenge Math class, and he'll admit: the shit really *was* a challenge. He was averaging high Bs but was determined to do better.

A week before The Math Test, Ms. Mays, Quan's favorite teacher on earth, went on maternity leave. (Quan still hasn't forgiven that damn baby for taking her away at such a critical point in his life.)

Before she left, she held Quan after class one day and told him how much she believed in him. That she couldn't wait to hear how well he did on the upcoming test. She knew he'd been struggling with the material, but, "I know *you* aren't gonna let this stuff get the best of you. *You*, Quan Banks, are gonna show those letters and numbers who's boss, am I right?"

And she smiled.

Even though it made him feel like a little-ass kid, Quan nodded. Because with her looking at him that way, like he could do *anything*, Quan wanted to prove her right.

It was the same way Daddy looked at Quan when Quan showed him that 100 percent he got on his contraction test in first grade.

Quan missed his dad.

Quan wanted to—*had* to—ace that damn algebra test.

So he studied. Hard.

Harder than he'd ever studied for anything in his life.

And you know what happened?

98%.

Quan almost lost his twelve-year-old MIND, he was so excited.

He floated through the rest of the day. Anticipating the moment he would show the test to Mama. The pride that would overtake her face. He'd show it to Dasia and Gabe and tell them it represented what could happen if they worked real hard and did their very best. Then he'd write Daddy a letter and he'd put it—with the test—in an envelope and he'd mail it to the address Daddy's lawyer gave Mama when he dropped by a few nights ago.

Yeah, the impromptu visit had *really* set Dwight off—

Your punk-ass son is enough of a reminder—
tell that nigga's attorney not to come by here
no more!

—but getting to send The Math Test to Daddy would make it all worth it.

As soon as Quan was off the bus, he broke into a sprint. Wanted to get home as fast as possible. He knew Mama would be home. She didn't leave the house when her body carried visible evidence of Dwight's "anger issues," and when Quan had left that morning, her wrist was in a brace and she could barely open her hand.

The test would lift her spirits too. Quan was sure of it. She'd see what he'd accomplished, and it would give her hope that things could get better. That he'd eventually be able to take care of her and Dasia and Gabe.

When he walked in the door, she was waiting for him.

"Ma, you'll never believe it—"

"You damn right I won't!"

The tiniest hole appeared in Quan's joy balloon as his mind kicked into gear, trying to figure out what she could be upset about. Had he left the bathroom light on again? He sometimes accidentally did that on mornings he had to get his siblings *and* himself ready for school and out the door on time. Their bus came thirteen minutes before his, so it was a lot to do.

But he remembered turning it off.

He hadn't put the milk in the fridge door—Dwight hated when he did that. And he'd made sure all of his socks were *in* the laundry basket.

So what could it be?

"I'm so disappointed in you, Junior," Mama continued, furious. "What do you have to say for yourself? Did you think they wouldn't call me?"

"Mama, I don't—"

"You had an algebra test yesterday, yes? Got it back today?"

Things were looking up! Quan straightened. "Yes, ma'am, I did, and I—"

"Cheated!"

The word was like a sucker punch. "Huh??"

"You heard me! Your teacher called. Told me you cheated on the test!"

"I didn't cheat, Ma!"

"Don't give me that BS, Junior! The man told me he *saw* you looking on a classmate's paper!"

Which . . . Quan couldn't deny. There was a point when he'd looked up and seen the brawny, neckless white man who looked more familiar with loaded-down barbells than linear inequalities glaring at him. But the sub had it all wrong. Said classmate was actually trying to cheat off *Quan*. He was an eighth-grade dude named Antwan Taylor. Bruh flat out whispered to ask Quan what answer he'd gotten for number six and then turned his paper so Quan could see the (wrong) answer Antwan had written.

"I really didn't cheat, Ma! I promise you!"

"Lemme see the test," she said.

Quan removed it from his bag. Held it out to her.

"Ninety-eight percent, huh?" She looked him right in the eye. "You really expect me to believe you didn't cheat, LaQuan?"

Quan couldn't believe what he was hearing. "Are you *serious?*"

"You ain't never brought nothin' higher than an eighty-seven percent up in here. I'm supposed to buy this sudden improvement hook, line and sinker, huh?"

"I *studied—*"

"Yeah. Your neighbor's paper."

"The MATERIAL, Ma! I studied the MATERIAL!"

"They gave you two days of in-school suspension. And you have to retake the test."

"But I didn't cheat, Ma!"

"Yeah, and *my* ass 'fell down the stairs.' " She held up her injured arm, and all Quan's other rebuttals got snatched right out of his throat.

His mouth snapped shut. Jaw clenched to keep it that way.

"If I ever hear about you cheating again, you can forget about this football shit you been on recently. Your ass will be on *lockdown*, you hear me?"

Quan's teeth ground into each other so hard, he wondered if they would break.

"I *said* DO YOU HEAR ME, LaQuan?"

Quan gulped. "Yes, ma'am."

35

"Get your ass outta my face and go 'study' for real this time."

Quan turned to head to his room, but her next words were like being shot with arrows from behind:

"And best *believe* your father is gonna hear about this. Might even send him the evidence of your indiscretion." Quan could hear the paper crinkle as she surely held it up in the air. "*Cheating.* I can't even believe you—"

And that was all he heard. Because in that moment everything crystallized for Vernell LaQuan Banks Jr.

It didn't matter what he did.

Staying focused didn't give Quan any control at all.

Snapshot:

One Boy Alone
in a Library
(2012)

The discovery that his favorite librarian is no longer at the branch—that she retired—is what pushes Quan over the edge. His last (relatively) safe-place gone.

And he knows it's gone because the lady now standing behind the main desk frowned at him when he came in, and a different lady has walked past the castle nook in the children's section where he's balled up with Unfortunate Events #13—*The End*—three times since he started chapter four.

And like . . . why? She think he's gonna steal damn *library books*? Stuff 'em in ziplock baggies and sell 'em outta his middle school locker for $10 a pop or something? *Get your dime-bag literature here!*

He turns a page.

This isn't a welcoming place. Not anymore.

It sucks.

He closes the book and grabs his backpack.

Walks out without a backward glance.

If nothing else, now they have a *reason* to give him dirty looks:

He left the book on the floor instead of putting it on the reshelving cart.

February 8

Dear Justyce,

First: yo, thanks for them graphic novel joints you sent. Them things have made me the coolest dude on the (cell)block. Everybody is especially into the black girl Iron Man ones. And the black Batman and black Robin one is also a hit.

I got your other "gift" as well. Bruh, what kinda dude sends a whole-ass teacher to his incarcerated homie like it's a box of commissary snacks? You clearly need to be president.

Anyway, I do have to admit: your boy Dr. Dray—"Doc," he said you call him (and I call him now too)—is pretty dope. He got on my nerves a little bit the first few times he came, asking all them damn questions and making me think about shit I didn't really want to. (Who the hell wants to sit around pondering all the ways this wack-ass country "is currently failing to uphold the standards set forth in its foundational documents"? That was a for-real question on one of the homework sheets!)

But then today he noticed your Martin notebook in my stack of stuff, and he started smiling. That's when he told me the truth: he'd been you and Manny's teacher, and you talked to him about me. About my other tutor deciding to quit on me.

I was mad at first knowing you told homeboy something I shared with you in confidence. But then I started really thinking about it, and I decided to write this letter. To thank you.

Well, partially to thank you.

The other part has to do with something Doc and I talked about in our class session today (and the fact that he said I should write to you about it).

Last time he was here, Doc brought this book for me to read. Native Son, it's called, and it's about this black dude who accidentally kills this white girl and then shoves her dead body in a furnace and starts a whole plot to try and blame her white boyfriend (shit's brutal, but roll with me). When he gets found out, he runs and tells HIS girl, but then panics and winds up killing her too.

They catch him, of course, and he's eventually convicted of murder and sentenced to death. (Bloop! SPOILER ALERT!) But the wildest part was even though it's set in like the 1930s or something, I really felt like I was reading a book about NOW.

Dude had all these obstacles he couldn't seem to get past no matter how hard he tried, and it was almost as though falling into the life of crime everybody expected from him was (sorta) unavoidable? I know it probably sounds crazy to an upstanding young gentleman such as yourself, but for real: based on the systems in place—the "institutions of oppression," as my former mentor, Martel, would say— homie's situation and how he ended up kinda seemed like destiny.

(Don't tell nobody I used the word "destiny.")

As I was telling Doc today, I could relate for real. I look back at my life, and though people like my wack-ass ex-counselor think I'm making excuses, I can't really see where I could've just "made different choices."

It's not like I didn't try. I remember this one time a teacher accused me of cheating because I got a good grade on a test. And my mama believed HIM. I know I also told you about that one prosecutor who called me a "career criminal" the second time I got arrested. I'd stolen one of this white dude's TWO phones. And only because I hoped to sell it so I could get my brother and sister some new shoes for school.

I reread your response to my very first letter where you admitted to busting up on some white boys at a party, and it made me wonder if that felt inevitable to you. I flipped back through the Martin journal, and there was even a reference to my cuzzo, may he rest in peace, using his fists at one point. Were these "incidents" bound to happen?

Anyway, I told Doc all this, and he goes, "Hmm," and rubbed his beardy chin all scholarly-like. Then he says, "So considering all that, would you say Bigger Thomas" (that's bruh from the book) "is a killer?"

"I mean, he definitely did some killing," I said, mulling it over, "but 'killer' just sounds so . . . malintentioned. Like it's something dude decided to do after giving it some serious thought."

Then he got me, J. Locked me in with them weird green-ass eyes and said: "What about you, Quan? Are YOU a killer?"

Thing is, I couldn't really answer. Part of me wanted to

flat out say "No, I'm not," but there was still this other voice saying "What if you are, LaQuan? What if it's inevitable?"

And of course "inevitability" isn't an excuse, and the consequences are (obviously) still the consequences, but I dunno. In a weird way, the whole shit makes me feel kinda better about my situation and how I got in it.

But it also makes me wonder: How did YOU do it, Justyce? I still remember when we met in that rocket ship (MY rocket ship that YOU invaded, by the way). We'd both left our houses after the streetlights were on because of stuff going on with our mamas. We grew up in the same area. Went to the same elementary and middle school. Even had a class or two together.

Why'd we turn out so different?

Was it "pure choice" like that counselor would say?

These questions are probably pointless now, but that's what's been going through my head.

Imma get back to this World of Wakanda joint you sent. I'll tell you one thing that's inevitable: pretty sure Ayo and Aneka are gonna hook up.

Looking forward to your next letter. (But you better not tell anybody I said that.)

Holler back at me,

Quan

3

Disrespect

Quan was hungry the First Time he did it. So were Dasia and Gabe.

It'd been a good year and a half since Dwight moved in, and Mama hadn't worked in four of those months. She said she'd been laid off, but Quan wasn't stupid. He knew one could only take so many "sick days" before a company decided to tell them to take off permanently.

In addition to taking his frustrations out on Mama, the COAN had started withholding access to money in response to "disrespect." (That's Count Olaf-Ass Negro, a name Quan secretly took to calling Dwight.) Anything could qualify: disagreeing with him in any way (this was the offense Mama was most often guilty of); moving something from where he'd left it (Quan's cardinal sin—which he couldn't seem to help after years of Mama drilling that "everything has a place" and "if you take it out, put it back!"); even failing to step over the groaning spot in the living room floor when he was watching TV.

Quan hated Dwight with every ounce of his being.

And Quan couldn't just take Dasia and Gabe and leave the house anymore: Dwight suddenly decided he didn't want **my damn kids spending too much time with Delinquent Junior.**

(Clearly Quan wasn't the only one in the house capable of negative nicknaming.)

Of course, if Quan disappeared by himself for too long, Dwight also felt disrespected. Which is how everything that led up to that First Time got started.

Mama had applied for *assistance* (she always said the word like she was trying not to gag on it as it left her throat), and they got a special debit card they could use at grocery stores—*EBT,* it was called. *Electronic Benefits Transfer.* Apparently back in the day, the system involved actual slips of money-sized paper everyone referred to as *food stamps.*

But she made the mistake of sending Dwight to the store with the card on one of the days she was incapacitated.

And he'd refused to give it back.

It was probably the Olaf-est thing he'd ever done at that point. He was controlling. Conniving. And based on something Quan overheard Dwight say that day—

I know you know where that son of a bitch was keepin' all his shit!

—Quan was convinced Dwight thought Mama had access to some treasure trove of cash and jewels that belonged to Daddy.

He needed a break, Quan did. From the shiver of unease that permeated the whole house like some awful supersonic vibration. From Dasia's newfound grown-ness to Gabe's insistence on being a baby brother-barnacle, gluing himself to Quan's side as often as possible. From Mama's anger-cloaked weariness. From Dwight's . . .

existence.

So he told Mama—who for the first time in weeks wasn't actively healing from a COAN encounter—that he was going out.

And he headed to his former favorite playground place.

Stepping over the latest evidence of unsavory activity inside his rocket ship (at least there wouldn't be any babies or diseases?), Quan climbed up to the observation deck. Largely to hide himself from anyone who might take issue with/make fun of an almost-thirteen-year-old hanging out in the grounded space vessel.

But once he got up there, Quan relaxed *so* much, he fell asleep.

And by the time he woke up—

the

   sun

      had

         gone

            down.

It was a cloudy night, so the streetlights—the ones that worked anyway—were his only source of illumination as he sprinted home. He wished they would all go out. That he could run straight into a darkness so thick and complete, it would swallow him whole.

Dwight wasn't there when Quan arrived.

But it didn't matter: the damage was already done.

Mama was on the couch, eyes glued to the television . . . which would've been unremarkable if not for the busted and puffy left side of her mouth and the fact that her left arm was cradled in her lap like she maybe couldn't use it.

Quan stopped a good distance away from her. He couldn't figure out what to think or how to feel. "Ma?"

She didn't respond. Didn't even shift her eyes away from the TV.

Quan dropped his own eyes. "Ma, I'm sorry. I fell asleep on the playground."

Nothing.

Quan sighed and forced his feet to carry him to his bedroom, where he *knew* he was gonna find something that would morph the guilt hanging over his head into something solid that would drop down onto his shoulders like a cape made of lead.

And he was right.

His siblings were in his closet.

Dasia was cradling Gabe, who'd fallen asleep. She wasn't

crying, but not three seconds after Quan pulled the door open, Gabe's body shuddered with an aftershock from what Quan could only assume was quite the sob session.

"Great, I can go to my room now," Dasia said, rolling her eyes as she shifted Gabe off her so she could get up.

Quan knew there was no point in asking her if she was okay. He knew all that attitude was her porcupine skin. Her way of letting people know they needed to

back

the

hell

up.

She shoved into his ribs in passing with her bony eight-year-old shoulder, and he took it. Absorbed that bit of her anger and let it throb without making a sound. He knew if he spat out the I'm sorry turning sour in his mouth, she would suck her teeth and say something like Don't nobody need your wack-ass apology, and right then, there was no way Quan could've dealt with how grown-up she was.

So he scooped Gabe up—little dude's body shook with another post-cry series of rapid-fire sniffles—carried him to his bed, and climbed in with him.

Dwight stayed gone for over a week.

Under normal circumstances, this would've made Quan the happiest dude maybe on all of earth.

But the COAN had taken the EBT card with him.

He'd also somehow found the minor cash stash Mama kept in one of the shoeboxes on the top shelf of her closet. There'd been a note in its place:

Oh, so now you keepin shit from me?
We gon see about that.

First few days, they were okay. They had Hawaiian rolls. Half a dozen eggs. Quarter jar of peanut butter. Two TV dinners and three pot pies in the freezer.

Day four, it got tight.

Day five, Dasia and Gabe split the final pot pie.

(Quan didn't eat.)

Gabe complained that he was still hungry, so Quan gave him the slice of crap pizza he'd smuggled from school.

(Quan stayed hungry.)

Day six, Quan smuggled home two slices.

And after getting Gabe in bed—Dasia plopped down on the couch, turned the TV on, and crossed her arms when Quan said it was time for bed (She was still hungry.)—Quan left the house.

He walked six minutes to a corner store he knew was owned by an elderly man who lived in the neighborhood. He'd been there a bunch of times, sent by Mama with $10 in his pocket to grab some milk or hot dogs or jelly when they were on the verge of running out.

Wasn't no money in his pocket now, but he went in anyway.

The old man smiled and waved at Quan as he entered. Then he excused himself and went to the bathroom.

Leaving the store wide open to Quan.

Trusting him.

As soon as the door to the storage room shut behind the old man, Quan gulped.

He looked left.

He looked right.

Then he grabbed a loaf of bread and a jar of peanut butter, and he walked out of the store.

His First Time.

Stealing.

Dasia cried as she bit into the peanut butter sandwich Quan handed her after waking her up. She'd fallen asleep in front of the TV.

Arms still crossed.

Day seven, the COAN came back.

With groceries.

Snapshot:

Two Boys Not Speaking
(2013)

It's not that Quan doesn't *like* his cousin Emmanuel.

He just don't know what the hell to say to the dude.

They occupy different universes, the boys do. Despite being blood. Emmanuel's—excuse him: *Manny's*—mama is Quan's mama's older half-sister. From what Quan understands, the two women didn't grow up together. His grandfather was apparently a bit of a "rolling stone," as Quan's mama put it, and *she*, Trish, was the product of one of said rolls into a different flower bed.

Granddad stayed with his original family, aka "Aunt Tiff" (Quan's never called her that. He's never called her anything.) and *her* mom.

Tiff hadn't even known Mama—Trish—existed until *Mama's*—Trish's—mama died and Tiff/Trish's shared daddy had a crisis of conscience and spilled the beans.

There was one time Mama had one glass of wine too many, and Tiff called to "check in." As soon as Mama hung up, she looked at Quan and said, "You ever wonder if my 'big sis'"—she'd used air quotes and everything—"only keeps in touch cuz she feels guilty about the fact that she had a daddy growing up, and I didn't?"

Quan didn't answer. He was eight at the time and had just returned from a weekend at *his* daddy's house.

Anyway.

Manny.

All Quan really knows is Manny's a year older and they have nothing in common.

They accidentally made eye contact once.

Quan looked away faster than the speed of light.

He's looked everywhere *but* at Manny since the two boys and their mamas took their seats around the table at this fancy-ass restaurant. Quan knows the place is *mad* fancy cuz the entire back wall where they're sitting is made of glass and he can see the smooth surface of a river just beyond it.

Shit is always fancy if it's on a river.

"You really *don't* have to cover us, Tiffany," Mama says.

"Nonsense," comes the reply. *Aunt* Tiff flicks the thought away like some irking insect, and the light catches on the boulder in her diamond ring.

Rings.

Cuz there's more than one.

"I haven't seen you in forever, baby sis," Tiff continues. "Lunch is the least I can do."

And it truly is. The least.

Quan knows Aunt Tiff and her husband got *mega* money. That they live out in Oak Ridge, which everybody knows is the most expensive part of Atlanta. That his cousin-he-don't-have-nothin'-to-say-to climbed out the passenger side of a Jag that *surely* has booty-warmers in the seats.

What would Manny say if he knew Mama's comment about Tiff not covering them was for show? They barely had food at *home*, so there's no way in *Quan's* universe they could afford to eat at this river restaurant.

Would big ballin' cuzzo bug out if he knew the real reason Mama's wearing a long-sleeved, turtleneck dress that goes down to her ankles when it's eighty-three degrees outside?

Quan knows Manny's dad is some financial investment big shot. Does Manny know Quan's daddy is locked up?

Quan is *sure* Manny's eyes would go all big if he knew Quan sometimes stole stuff. That Manny's butt would clench up and all the moisture would leave his mouth (with them white-ass, straight-ass, perfect-ass teeth) if he knew that the moment Quan saw the ice on "Aunt Tiff's" fingers and wrists, his mind started calculating. Running through all the stuff he could afford for himself and his siblings with just *one* of her rings. Quan has never stolen jewelry or anything with value like that before, but still.

Different universes.

The food arrives: sweet potato fries and a lamb burger for Quan (without the *fig jam* and *goat cheese* that were supposed to be on it, because what even *is* that shit and why would *anyone* put it on a burger?).

Asparagus (gross), some creamy white stuff that ain't mashed potatoes, and a hunk of pink fish with the silvery skin still on top for Manny.

Salmon, Quan remembers. Because Manny ordered it without even looking at the menu.

This clearly isn't Manny's first time at the river restaurant. But Quan's 98 percent sure it'll be his (Quan's) last.

Quan sighs.

Manny does too.

But they don't see each other.

And they certainly don't speak.

4

Defiance

The only other time in his life Quan felt fear as mind-numbing as the night they took Daddy? His own first arrest.

The whole thing was so ridiculous. He was thirteen. Eighth grade.

(Which he barely made it into. Looking back, it's wild to Quan how drastically shit had changed inside him.)

On this particular day, he was just . . . mad.

It got like that sometimes. Nothing had to happen—or *trigger*, as Doc says when Quan slips up and starts talking about his feelings. There were just days, moments, when rage would overtake him and his vision would literally go white at the edges.

Quan wasn't a violent dude. Yeah, he'd been in a fight here and there, especially when kids would talk shit about Daddy being locked up. But he wasn't one to explode: screamin' and cussin', hulkin' out, flippin' tables, throwin' chairs and swingin' on teachers like this one dude in his class, DeMarcus, who got expelled a month before Quan's (dumb) arrest.

No. That wasn't Quan.

Instead—he stole.

Never anything major. Some days he'd swipe a pencil from a classmate's desk or grab one of the markers from the metal tray beneath the crusty old dry-erase board. He'd tail a mom and kid into Rite Aid just close enough for it to look like he was with them, then he'd slip off and pocket a tin of Altoids or a fresh tube of Burt's Bees lip balm. He'd get the double tingle with that one . . . one in his fingertips as he made the grab, and another on his lips once he applied the stuff.

Magic.

On THE day, he was particularly furious. His eyes burned with it, and his ears rang, and for hours, he'd had the taste of metal in his mouth.

The convenience store he walked into wasn't new, but it'd been remodeled. There were flashy new gas pumps—they had *diesel* now—and a bright new sign. The storefront had new windows and doors Quan was sure were bulletproof, and on the inside, the back wall was inset with new slushy (*twelve* flavors), soda, juice, and coff-uccin-cciato machines.

Real shiny.

While the snack aisle was tempting, Quan found himself drawn to an end-of-the-aisle display filled with . . . *novelties* is the only way to describe it. There were something called *Pez*, which looked like weird toys but apparently involved candy.

There were bags of variously colored marbles. There were packages of dice and oddly shaped lighters. There was even some . . . paraphernalia. Brightly colored glass pipes and bowls.

What caught Quan's eye? A deck of playing cards.

To this day, he has no idea why. There was nothing special about them. There were three or four full decks at home, so it's not like he was getting anything he didn't have.

He just knows they called to him. Beckoned. His fingertips got to tingling.

He checked all around to make sure no one was looking—outside of an older woman buying cigarettes and a baby-toting mom grabbing a Sprite, he was the only one in the store. Then he grabbed a pack of the cards and slipped them into his pocket.

He thought he was in the clear, Quan did. He even popped into the bathroom to make it look like his reason for being in the building was a need to pee.

But on his way out, the brown-skinned (but definitely not black) clerk stopped him.

"Young man . . ."

And Quan turned.

"Don't move any further," the dude said. "I'm calling the police."

He had his hands on the counter. One of them around the handle of a gun.

. . .

He never pointed the pistol at Quan. Just kept it where Quan could see it.

What Quan hadn't realized—and felt stupid about later: the fancy remodel came with a fancy security system. One with cameras. So the clerk could watch just about *everything* happening in the store on a screen behind the (definitely bulletproof) glassed-in checkout area.

He saw Quan pocket the cards.

Which . . . was it *that* big of a deal? They were $2.99. He could put 'em back, promise to leave and never return, and be on his way.

Did dude really have to call the damn cops over a

    deck

        of

           Bicycle

              playing

                cards?

That **can't-do-shit** rage expanded in Quan's chest and pushed up into his throat, but he couldn't get his mouth open to let it out, so it whistled up past his ears and tried to make its escape through the inside corners of his eyes.

But he wasn't about to let himself cry. Not with a dude mad over three-dollar cards staring him down like he'd busted in with a mask and a Glock and tried to rob the place.

"Hey, man, can we just forget this? I don't even need the cards, I can put them ba—"

But then the bell connected to the door chimed, and in stepped a police officer who looked like someone had stuck a bicycle-pump tube in his rear and

        pump

          pump

            pumped

    him up.

Perhaps even using the air that had been in Quan's lungs: he suddenly didn't have any left.

He locked eyes with the cop, and the Bad (Dad) Night washed over him, and his chest

locked up

the way it had when kid-snatcher cop had Quan's scrawny eleven-year-old torso wrapped in that death grip.

Wasn't the best time for it either. Swole Cop took Quan's inability to answer questions—

    We got a problem here, son?

      You hear me talkin' to you?

        So you're a tough guy then?

          Not gonna answer my questions?

—as an act of defiance.

Quan found air the moment Swole Cop's ham-ish hand locked around Quan's (still scrawny) upper arm in a death grip. Sucked that air in with *gusto* as he gasped from the sudden burst of pain.

And then he let it out.

"OWW!"

"So now you can speak?"

He jerked Quan around and snatched him out of the store with more force than necessary considering Quan wasn't resisting in the least. He was too scared.

He blinked and saw Daddy's body go limp.

When they reached the squad car, the guy shoved Quan against it and yanked his hands behind his back.

Then dude put Quan in handcuffs.

And for the second time since pre-k,

Quan wet his pants.

Swole Cop spun him around.

And noticed.

"Did you just piss yourself?"

The tears started then.

What would Mama say? Was there a way to keep Dwight from finding out Quan got himself arrested? He'd certainly see this as "disrespect."

What would Dasia think? She definitely had opinions now—and would certainly share hers with Quan when she found out about this.

And then there was Gabe. Despite having way fewer damns to give than in the past, this wasn't exactly the example Quan wanted to set for his baby bro . . .

"Whatcha cryin' for, huh?" Swole Cop spat. "Not so tough now, are ya? You delinquents strut around like you own the goddamn world—"

"It was just a deck of cards!"

"Deck of cards today, some lady's purse tomorrow. Get your ass in the car."

And he opened the back door and pushed Quan in.

Two hours, Quan was at the precinct.

Alone.

In a room with a table and two chairs and a mirror he was pretty sure was a window from the other side—he'd watched plenty of *Law & Order: SVU.*

The cuffs had been undone for all of fifteen seconds so they could take his backpack off, but then Swole Cop just cuffed him in the front. Led him to the sterile-ass space, plopped him in a chair, and left the room.

Nothing but his churning thoughts, gnawing fear, and growing rage to keep him company.

How had he even gotten there? What was he supposed to do? Was anybody coming for him? Would he go to jail? Would that mean arraignment-indictment-plea-trial-verdict-sentencing . . . all the stuff Daddy had to go through?

It was a *deck of cards.*

Cards.

Fifty-four.

Stacked.

Against him.

Four suits.

Two jokers.

63

Joke . . .

    was on him.

What was he supposed to **do**?

  . . . *good in school*

    got him a cheating accusation and in-school
    suspension.

  . . . *his very best*

    wasn't ever good enough.

  . . . *what he could*

    felt as limited as his hands did in the cuffs.

What

    Was

        Quan

            Supposed

                To

                    Do?

Mama wasn't gonna get rid of Dwight no matter how often he hurt her (though Quan didn't get *WHY*), but Quan knew telling somebody else would not only hurt *her*, but him and Dasia and Gabe too. Because they'd get taken away.

Split up for sure.

Both of Mama's folks were gone, so Quan would probably go to some random relative of Daddy's he'd never met (since Daddy's folks were also deceased).

No clue what would happen with Dasia and Gabe. Quan wasn't sure Dwight actually had parents—seemed more likely he was the spawn of demons or the result of some test tube experiment gone wrong—so whether there were family members they could go to on *their* dad's side, he didn't know.

Only *shared* living relative Quan could think of was "Aunt" Tiff, and though she seemed nice, he doubted she'd want to open her nice-ass house to three little hood kids (though he didn't doubt she had the spare rooms). He was sure his salmon-on-a-river-eating cousin didn't want anything to do with the likes of him.

And wasn't a damn thing he could do about it. About *any* of it.

He was in a police station.

In handcuffs.

Arrested.

The deck of cards he slid into a pocket sealing his fate.

"Delinquent Junior,"

Dwight had been calling him for years.

Was that who he was for real?

There was no denying the impulse to take what wasn't his. Was the D in his DNA for *delinquent*? The Jr. shorthand of "Junior" for *just repeating*?

Maybe Daddy had been wrong. Ms. Mays too.

There was no way out.

No way up.

Maybe a way *through* . . . but he had no idea what to.

Could he really *be* anyone different than who he was?

Who even *was* he?

The door to the room opened, and an officer in slacks and a button-down, badge clipped to his belt, stood aside so a brown-skinned woman wearing dark sunglasses could lean her upper body into the room.

"Let's go" was all Mama said.

And as she and Quan stood waiting for a cop who clearly was in no rush to retrieve Quan's meager-ass belongings, the doors to the lobby opened, and a commotion ensued.

There was shouting—

> *"Man, get your filthy hands OFF me. I ain't even do nothin'!"*

—then feet shuffling and a bit of a struggle as two cops pulled a darker-than-Mama brown-skinned boy into the booking area. He wasn't quite kicking and screaming, but—

> *"Y'all always be comin' at me! Tryna pin some shit on me!"*

"Let's go, LaQuan." (From Mama.)

> *"Get on my damn nerves!"*

That's when the boy—because he was definitely a *boy*; maybe a year or two Quan's senior: age fifteen at most—caught sight of Quan.

And smiled.

> *"Hey, I know you!"*

he shouted across the space.

And he did. Quan knew him too.

Well, knew *of* him.

66

Quan wasn't completely sure of his name—either *Dre* or *Trey*—but he'd definitely seen him around the neighborhood.

One particular instance came to mind: one of the last times Quan was permitted to take Dasia and Gabe to the playground, he'd seen one guy—definitely older—duck out of the rocket ship with a black book bag slung over his shoulder. Quan could see inside then, and there was another guy counting money.

A boy.

He'd looked up, and Quan froze.

Money-counting boy had just smirked. Like *he* was the new captain of Quan's spaceship.

Same way he was now smirking at Quan in the precinct.

"See you on the outside, homie," he said.

Then he quit resisting the cops and disappeared.

March 12

Dear Justyce,

Bruh.

I think I might be in love.

Her name is Liberty Ayers. Gorgeous, long dreadlocks.
Eyes so dark they're almost black. Skin the color of a roasted
hazelnut. (But don't tell her I said that shit cuz when I
mentioned it to her—and you know your boy mentioned it to
her—she looked me dead in my eye and said, "You're childish.
Women don't like being compared to food.")

I'm not gonna talk about her body cuz she caught me
checkin' her out and "read me the riot act," as Doc said later
when I told him how homegirl lit into me. But I will say, if I WAS
gonna talk about it, I'd be saying some excellent things.

I can't ask her to marry me yet because she's my case
manager's intern, so it would create a "conflict of interests."
(Again: Doc's words.) But talking to her makes me wonder how
different my life coulda been if I'd met somebody like HER
instead of Trey at thirteen.

She's his same age—nineteen going on twenty—and a
sophomore at Emory University. Now. When she was younger,
though? Homegirl was a menace.

And her story . . . Looking at her, you would never expect it. She was raised by her granddaddy cuz both parents were locked up, but he had real bad diabetes and was wheelchair-bound, so she did more taking care of him than the other way around.

Actually messed me up a little bit hearing her talk about her younger self because she sounded a lot like my baby sister.

Anyway, Libz (you ain't allowed to call her that, though) started getting into fights and shit in third or fourth grade. First time locked up, she was twelve . . . fight went too far and she broke some girl's arm (BRUH!).

Second time was for second-degree criminal damage to property.

Third time? Grand theft auto.

At fourteen.

(BRUUUUUUH!!!)

But she said something that got me: the twelve months she had to serve for that final offense were some of the hardest but BEST months of her life. She lost her granddad and everything, but she said even THAT made her wanna make some changes. And all because she met someone who wouldn't let her "continue to bury my bright spots," as she put it. (She got a way with words too, dawg. Total package.)

Now while I'm not buying all the happy-happy-joy, *meet-one-person-and-turn-your-life-around!* bullshit, it got me thinking about my own situation. I do think me winding up in here was inevitable, but now I can't stop pondering, if you will, all these what-ifs.

Did you know the first time Trey and I ever spoke, we were at the police station? He was being booked, and I was being released. STILL mad about the dumb shit they arrested me for, but he was there because of a breaking and entering charge.

After he was let go—because in that case, he hadn't actually done it—he sought me out. And even though I knew his ass was trouble, I started kicking it with him. Going wherever he asked me to.

Listening to Liberty talk, I feel like I started to get why. She was telling me how HER case manager—the one who helped her make a turnaround—taught her that people have this drive to do stuff so other people know we exist.

(Bet you forgot a dude was smart, didn't you? #GotEem!)

It really made me think about the years between being a KID kid—like that age when you and me met—and a for-real grown-ass man (even though when you black, SOME folks wanna act like you're a grown-ass man before you actually are). How when you're in that like middle to high school range, the people you're connected to REALLY influence what you wind up doing.

After my dad got locked up, I ain't really have no positive connections—nobody who was a good influence or who called out some good they saw inside me. Honestly, except for ONE teacher—who just had to go and have a baby—wasn't nobody

70

paying me no mind AT ALL, let alone saying anything positive or uplifting or encouraging or pick your feel-good term.

Which I think is where Trey came in for me. Nah, he wasn't no good influence, but he did . . . see me. If that makes any sense. Libz's life shifted to its current direction because somebody saw HER and like noticed the GOOD shit in her. Started pointing it out.

A positive connection, she called it.

Which makes me wonder: Would MY life have gone in a different direction if I'd made more positive connections? Cuz Trey was really just the first in a string of NOT-positive connections that led to some not-great decisions.

Don't make no difference now because here I am. But "food for thought" (#ShitDocSays) nonetheless.

Yo, speaking of Doc, homie has really grown on me.

It's too bad I didn't meet him sooner.

—Q

5

Delinquent

Trey was waiting for Quan inside the rocket ship.

How he'd known Quan would eventually come there is still a mystery to Quan, but three days after their brief encounter at the precinct—if you could even call it that—Quan stepped onto the playground intending to vanish into his personal outer space

and

found

Montrey David Filly.

Sitting.

Back pressed up against the curved inner wall. Long legs outstretched and crossed at the ankles. Hands clasped over his midsection.

Chillin'.

Quan stopped dead the moment he saw Trey in there. He was still a good few yards from the rocket.

Which didn't matter at all.

"Took you long enough," the older boy quipped, smile

slanted. A wicked glint in his eye. "I been comin' here every day."

Which gave Quan pause . . . but also made him feel kinda good? "You were looking for me?"

Trey rolled his eyes. "Man, get your little ass in here," he said.

And Quan went.

Trey couldn't have known it (or maybe he could've?), but in *that* moment, Quan didn't actually want to be alone.

He needed a friend.

Someone who cared.

Because from the moment Mama and Quan had stepped out of the fluorescent-lit law-and-order lair into the crisp Georgia evening, it was crystal clear to Quan that she no longer did.

For the first ten of the fifteen-minute bus ride home, they hadn't exchanged a single word. In fact, Quan wondered if it looked like they were even together. He'd been his mother's son for thirteen years and knew when her refusal to look at him was rooted in anger. *That* felt like sitting next to a dragon whose hide was radiating heat because it was fighting

hard

to keep the fire in.

This, though? It'd been like he wasn't even there.

There was no heat of motherly fury. No fire at all.

There was . . . ice.

73

And it got colder and colder—the void growing larger and larger—the closer they got to home.

When the bus took the turn before the turn before their stop, Quan had literally shivered. Little hairs on his arms raised up and everything.

"Mama, I'm sorry," he'd said, eyes fixed on what looked like a wad of gum so stomped into the grooved floor, it'd become a part of it.

She'd reached up and pulled the stop-cord that wrapped around the interior of the bus.

"That's what your father used to say."

Then she'd stood up and walked to the rear exit door.

That's how things continued over the next few days. Dwight had vanished again (though Quan was sure he'd come back eventually) so it was more peaceful around the house . . . but Mama wouldn't even look in his direction. She wouldn't speak unless spoken to, and then only with short, emotionless responses—

Yeah.

Nope.

Dunno.

and then Quan's least favorite:

I don't care, LaQuan.

Dasia followed her lead.

Gabe still loved Quan, but he was also afraid. Of what, Quan didn't know, but the fact that the little dude would check to see if Mama or Dasia was around before interacting with his big bro felt like a stab straight to the heart with a Lego sword.

Quan was utterly and completely alone.

(Over a deck of damn cards.)

"You not gone cry, are you?" Trey asked as Quan sat down beside him, more than ready to blast off into oblivion.

Quan dropped his eyes and shook his head. "Nah."

"It's cool if you do," Trey said. "I ain't gone tell nobody—"

And he shrugged.

"—I cried after my first arrest."

Quan sniffled then. And hated himself for it.

"I get it, li'l man," Trey went on. "First time is scary as fuck."

"Yeah."

"I was eleven. Damn cuffs barely fit."

Silence.

(Quan didn't really know what to do with that information.)

"I seent your mom's demeanor," Trey continued. "She not really speakin' to you now, right?"

Quan sighed. "Yeah."

"Mines was the same way. Your pops locked up?"

Crazy. "Yeah."

"Figured."

"What'd you do?" Quan asked, not really thinking. "When you were eleven?"

"Skippin' school and an MIP."

"MIP?"

"Minor in possession of alcohol. I did this pretrial diversion shit that included Al-Anon meetings—they wanted me to 'see how alcoholism affects other people'—so they wound up dropping the charges, but the arrest itself? Scariest shit I ever been through, man."

"How old are you now?"

"Fifteen. You what, twelve?"

"Just turned thirteen."

"It's crazy, ain't it? I had this white lawyer once—really wanted to *help* kids like us, so he took my case pro bono. I was thirteen at the time, and he told me he had a son my age who'd just had his bar mitzvah, you familiar?"

Quan shook his head. "Nah."

"It's this ceremony where a young Jewish dude becomes 'accountable for his actions.'" He used air quotes. "So he goes from 'boy' to 'man,' essentially. Lawyer homie is sitting there all geeked, telling me about it, and I'm thinking to myself: So your son is a grown man by Jewish standards, yet still gets treated like a kid. Meanwhile ain't no ceremonies for kids like us, but if *we* get in trouble we get treated like adults."

Nothing Quan could say to that.

"Funniest part is the only reason dude was even workin' with me is because I got caught with a dime—that's a little baggie of weed that costs ten bucks—"

"I know what a *dime* is, man."

Trey smirked. "Yeah, all right. Well, like I was saying, as the cop frisked me, he said, 'You wanna act like an adult, the law will treat your ass like one.' When I asked lawyer dude if he'd ever say anything like that to his son, he was shook."

So was Quan.

"Anyway, you in it now, li'l dude."

Quan swallowed hard. Was he *in it*? What did that actually mean?

"I gotchu, though, all right?" Trey threw an arm around Quan's shoulders then. "I been where you at, man. And I know where you goin'. Ain't a whole lotta pathways for niggas like us, you feel me?"

And Quan did.

Feel him.

So when Trey would come a-knockin', Quan would always go.

While that first arrest did wind up on Quan's record, no charges were filed.

With the second arrest, he got lucky (and Trey did too because the boys had just parted ways): he *was* charged—juvenile possession of a firearm . . . not that he had any intention of using the .22 caliber he'd gotten from Trey that was about the size of his palm—but it was a misdemeanor. The juvenile court district attorney was two hearings from retirement and wanted "to go out on a restorative note," so she dropped the charges, gave Quan community service, and told him to get his life together

"before it's too late, young man."

The charge attached to his third arrest stuck—breaking and entering tended to do that—and Quan did his first ninety-day stint in a youth detention center.

He spent his fourteenth birthday there.

But looking back, it was the fourth arrest that solidified his course.

He was at the mall. Group of white dudes in suits were laughing all loud and shit in the food court. Which irritated Quan: if it'd been a group of dudes like him, seated in the same positions, talking and cackling at the same volume, they would've been asked to leave.

Once his eyes caught on the *two* phones in the open bag of the dude seated at the head of the table—Idiot.—the irritation made it that much easier to decide on the bump-and-snatch move he

(thought he'd)

perfected.

Perfect diversion—lady pushing a stroller—

went by at the perfect time.

Bump . . .

Quan—

tripped

ceremoniously and the single wheel on the front of the stroller hit the table just as he'd planned.

"Oh my goodness, ma'am!"

And he straightened quickly, slipping the extra phone in his pocket on his way up.

"I'm so sorry!"

Lay it on thick,

Trey had told Quan.

Really sell it.

And he did. He *swears* he did. The lady was asking if *he* was okay.

He made it out the mall and halfway up the hill to the bus stop. But then a small SUV pulled up alongside him.

Mall security.

Petty theft was the charge.

Delinquent was the proclamation. (After
    career criminal, of course.)
        Twelve months in a regional youth detention
            center was the sentence.

And Quan came out . . . different.

Enlightened. To darkness. His own, and how it
                                affected things.

There was Antoine (about as dark as him), age thirteen—doing eight months on an aggravated assault charge.

DeAngelo (a little darker), age fifteen—ten months on "trafficking of a controlled substance."

Alejandro (not as dark, but still brown), age twelve—twelve months on "participating in criminal gang activity." (And he hadn't actually done anything. *Guilty by association.*)

And then there was White Boy Shawn (Black Boy Shawn—sixteen—was headed to a juvenile section of the adult prison for his involvement in a drive-by shooting that left two guys dead).

Seventeen.

Stabbed his dad eight times with a butcher
   knife.

While the man was sleeping.

Shawn's final charge and sentence?

Simple assault. Sixty days.

And **not even** in detention. At a

Youth Development Campus.

There was a part of Quan that wished his awareness had a knob he could just crank down to zero.

But for Vernell LaQuan Banks Jr., there was no

not noticing

the number of brown faces

   that came and stayed

      compared to the number of **not-brown** ones

         that came and left.

Twelve months in before he was out.

And Trey had also had an interesting year.

His grandma had passed.

   And his mom hadn't taken it well.

   (So he hadn't either.)

When he tripped over a desk at school and it was discovered that the clear liquid in the bottle he constantly swigged from *wasn't* water, they expelled him.

(He'd been on his final strike.)

(Not that he really gave a damn about
school.)

(Or so he said.)

"That was the final straw for Moms," Trey told Quan as they sat outside the rocket ship—they'd gotten taller and couldn't both fit inside anymore—passing a vape back and forth between them.

(That was another thing: Quan had sworn off
blunts. Something about *carcinogens*.)

"Her ass moved to Florida and wouldn't take
me with her."

"Wait, for real?"

inhaaaale . . .

exhaaaaaale.

"Yup."

"Damn, bruh. So where you livin' now?"

inhaaaale . . .

exhaaaaaale.

"Here and there. Speakin' of which—" Trey looked at a watch on his wrist. "I gotta go meet my boys." It was . . . sparkly.

Trey noticed Quan noticing.

"Shit fire, ain't it?" He turned the thing back and forth so it caught the light.

"Where'd you get it?"

"New, uhh . . . business venture," Trey said, pushing to his feet. "Matter fact—" He looked down at Quan. Rubbed the patch of hairs that had appeared on his chin since Quan last saw him.

He looked a little too *calculating* for Quan's liking in that moment, and Quan's muscles tensed of their own accord. It'd been a long time since Quan was in the presence of someone he considered a *friend*. He didn't really know how to act.

Trey nodded. "Yeah," he said, answering a question Quan wasn't privy to. "Come on."

"Where we going?"

Trey smiled. "It's some folks I want you to meet."

Snapshot:

A Boy Meeting a Man
(2016)

Quan is nervous as hell walking up the "Hallowed Hallway," as he's heard the guys call it. He's been on the porch before, but to be invited inside?

Huge.

It's different than he expected, though he can't articulate how, even in his mind. He's been kicking it with Trey and them for a minute now, and has pieced together bits about the inner workings of their crew and their operation. But seeing framed images of ancient Egyptian kings and queens hung across from a poster that reads *The racist dog policemen must withdraw immediately from our communities, cease their wanton murder and brutality and torture of black people, or face the wrath of the armed people. —Huey Newton* . . .

Well, Quan don't really know what to make of that.

There's no one in the living room when he gets to it, but within a couple seconds, a deep—and he'll admit: *smooth*—voice comes from somewhere else in the house:

"Have a seat, young brutha. I'll be with you in a minute."

Quan does as he's told, choosing a spot on a well-worn sofa. Then he takes in the room. It smells . . . flowery? Quan is suddenly smacked with a memory of the first time he stepped into Ms. Mays's classroom in seventh grade. The scent inside was so different from anything he'd ever smelled before, it made him feel like he'd stepped into another world, as corny as that sounds.

Turns out, Ms. Mays had this flower-shaped device plugged into her wall that had these interchangeable glass bulb joints filled with liquid fragrance.

Quan spots one sticking out of an outlet opposite him.

And now he's *really* confused. Especially since it's plugged in beneath a framed poster of a beret-wearing dude sitting on what looks like a woven throne. Homie's holding a spear in one hand and a shotgun in the other.

"Quan, right?"

Quan jumps and a yelp slips past his lips.

Standing beside him—and chuckling—is a bearded brown-skinned dude in white pants and a V-neck shirt that looks like it came straight outta Africa. He hands Quan a glass bottle, then goes to sit in a round chair that looks like it's made of bamboo. He's holding a glass bottle too.

Quan peeks at the label on the one in his hand: JAMAICAN GINGER BREW.

"Drink up," the man says.

So Quan does. It's . . . good. Kinda spicy, but also soothing in a weird way. He relaxes a little.

"That your given name?" the man asks.

"Huh?"

"Quan. That's what's on your birth certificate?"

Quan shakes his head. "No, sir."

"Dispense with the *sir*, little homie. You can call me *Martel* or *Tel*. Take your pick. What's your given name?"

"Uhh—" And Quan falters. He never tells *anyone* his given name. "The whole thing?"

Martel chuckles again. "Every part that's given."

"Vernell LaQuan Banks Jr."

"Junior, huh? So you got your daddy's name?"

"Yeah." And Quan drops his eyes.

"I'll take it he ain't in the picture?"

"He's incarcerated."

"And you?"

"Huh?"

"You been incarcerated?"

Now Quan's jaw clenches. "Yeah."

"You mad about it?"

This gives Quan pause. It's a question no one's ever asked him, case managers included. He meets Martel's gaze. "Yeah," he says. "I am."

"Why? You did the crime, didn't you?"

Now Quan gulps. Last thing he wants to do is start sounding like some of the dudes in lockup who constantly complained about how "unfair" the system is. "Always take responsibility for your actions, Junior," Daddy used to say. "I know the potential consequences of what I do, and I choose to do it anyway, so if it comes down on me, I don't get to complain."

But that was the thing: as uncomfortable as the complaints always made him, Quan couldn't deny their ring of truth. The system *is* unfair. Quan saw that with his own eyes. Hell, he lived it.

"I mean, I did, but"—he fumbles around in his head for the right words—"they gave me a YEAR in detention for trying to steal a cell phone. Which, yes, was wrong . . ." Quan's mind flashes to White Boy Shawn, aka the Dad Stabber. "And I'm not *complaining* about having to suffer some consequences for my wrongdoing. Just seems like the 'time' was . . . excessive. Considering the 'crime.'"

Martel's eyes narrow just the slightest bit, but it doesn't give a single clue as to what he's thinking.

"What else you mad about?" he says.

That's certainly not what Quan was expecting. "What you mean?"

"You what? Fifteen?"

"Yeah."

Martel nods. "My master's thesis was on the trajectories of African American adolescent males raised in impoverished urban environments by single mothers."

Which . . . "HUH?"

Now Martel laughs in earnest. "I got a master's degree in social work, li'l man. Dudes like you are my 'area of expertise,' if you will, and frankly, the shit I learned is the reason I came back home and do what I do now. You know who that is?" He nods toward the poster with beret guy.

"Nah," Quan replies.

"That's Huey Newton. One of the cofounders of the Black Panther Party for Self-Defense. I came across a quote of his while working on my thesis: *Black Power is giving power to people who have not had power to determine their destiny.* And there it was: a summation of my research findings, and what I needed to do about it. So I'll ask you again: What else you mad about, Vernell?"

Quan is stunned. Not only by the blatant use of his "given" name, but also by just about every word that came out of Martel's mouth. Quan is *fully* aware of what Martel does now, and he'd be lying if he said he was expecting dude to be college-educated. Also, that quote hit Quan right in the chest.

But where does he even begin?

"Start with home," Martel says as if Quan's question has appeared on his forehead. "I know you been spendin' a good bit of time with my guys. Which means home ain't really a place you wanna be, am I right?"

Now Quan has a knot in his throat. When he left "home" this morning, Mama and Dwight were all boo'd up on the couch, watching TV. Mama with a fading bruise on her left jaw and her wrist in a brace that got *way* too much use from a person who didn't play sports or have carpal tunnel.

Shit was sickening.

And he tells Martel so.

He tells Martel everything. (Almost.)

At one point Martel goes to get him another ginger brew, but this time he gives it to Quan iced in a glass with something bitter added that burns a bit going down but makes his muscles unclench.

When Quan is done, Martel tells him how the organization functions and offers Quan an in, provided he can abide by the rules.

(Quan does notice there's no explanation of what happens if one *breaks* said rules, and it does make him hesitate—but only for a second.)

And then he's in. Just like that.

"So I'll see you at Morning Meeting tomorrow, eight a.m. sharp," Martel says as they both rise to their feet. It's a statement, not a question. And that's when Quan realizes there's no turning back.

So . . . he leans in. "Tel, can I ask you something?" he says.

Martel slips his hands into his pockets and lifts his chin. "Whassup?"

"That, uhh . . ." and Quan gestures to the fragrance diffuser plugged in beneath Sir Huey. "Which scent is it?"

At this, Martel smiles so bright, Quan has to look away. "It's Spring Sunrise."

Quan nods, now filled with some emotion he can't name. "That's what I thought," he says. "I'll, uhh . . . see you in the morning."

He heads back up the hallway and out the door.

April 4

Dear Justyce,

Yo, so when Doc was here earlier (picking apart my <u>Native Son</u> vs. <u>Invisible Man</u> essay, the chump), he told me today is the anniversary of Dr. MLK's assassination. Which of course made me think of your punk ass. ☺

(Yeah, I drew a li'l smiley face. So what?)

In your last letter to me, you asked why I joined the Black Jihad. And to be honest, the question irritated me. So I wasn't gonna answer.

But then I got to thinkin' about the whole assassination thing.

Sidenote: you ever notice that word begins with "ass" twice? I wonder if that mean something etymologically. Bet you ain't know I knew THAT word, sucka!

(Real talk: Doc got my ass prepping for a "practice" SAT. Which I can't believe I agreed to do. Dude is persuasive as shit.)

Anyway, Doc was tellin' me more about King's life and how a lady tried to kill my mans in 1958 with a letter opener (!!) at a book signing (!!!!!). In addition to helping me make the firm decision that I never want to be an author (bruh!), talking

91

about Dr. King made me think of that one real short letter you wrote to him in your notebook right after Manny passed. The one when you lamented the fact that Manny hadn't never done nothing wrong, but he lost his life anyway.

Which made me think about your question. Because really, the shit that happened to MLK and to Manny—what happens to good dudes all the time—played a big role in my decision.

Not those things directly (I obviously joined before what happened to Manny), but the fact that they happen at all. That a dude just tryna get equal rights for folks can get taken out. That a kid who ain't never even done nothing criminal can get taken out.

And then the fact that niggas like me and Trey who DO do wrong get punished more harshly than white kids who do the same shit? If Brock or Conrad steals a cell phone in the mall, they get a finger wagged in they face and gotta volunteer in a soup kitchen a couple times. I get branded a "career criminal" and locked up with the key thrown out. I know I told you about the dude who stabbed his pops, but bruh, if I had a dollar for every white boy I've seen come into detention and leave within a couple days—both back when I was fourteen AND now—I could prolly buy my way out this bitch.

Shit's wack, Justyce.

Anyway, after seeing that shit happen over and over, then getting out and coming "home" and finding nothing changed there, I guess I was just fed up. Stayed in school cuz "truancy" was a probation violation that would've landed my ass on house arrest (definitely a no-go), but having that "Delinquent" on my record made folks treat me different even though I stayed caught up while I was in and did my work (well) once I got out.

My mama had her own shit going on. And I hadn't heard from my dad since he went in. I sent him letters for like the first six months he was locked up, and even one while I was, but he never responded.

I just ain't really have nobody in my corner, Justyce. I think that's why your question rubbed me the wrong way. Like how could YOU possibly understand? I know shit with your dad wasn't . . . "Optimal" feels like a good word. But I remember your moms vividly, and she wasn't 'bout to let you mess up. You went to that fancy-ass school and had all type of support . . . How could you possibly understand the inner workings of a hood cat like me?

But thinking about you and about Manny and Dr. King after Doc left today . . . it's a pretty significant gap between that letter where you basically gave up, and the one you wrote when you got to Yale. I know you came to visit ME somewhere in between there, and you weren't doing so hot. Not sure if you ever used that number I gave you (kinda surprised you haven't mentioned it), but as I was sitting here pondering, I thought to myself maybe—JUST maybe—I wasn't giving you the benefit of the doubt.

So.

The reason I joined the Black Jihad: I needed backup.

Support without judgment. People who hadn't—and wouldn't—
give up on me.

I needed a family.

And it wasn't all bad like people assume. It wasn't all
about turf and crime and bullshit like that. Martel is a
visionary. His grand plan involves building a community
center and opening a bookstore in our neighborhood. He
wanted to help people.

It was a dope-ass thing to be a part of.

Yeah, I'm in here now and prolly ain't getting out no time
soon, and yeah, that happened sooner than I anticipated . . .

But at least I'm alive.

That may not seem like much to you, but it's more than I
thought possible.

It's also more than either Manny or Dr. King can say.

I do hope you're keeping that Dream alive, though.

Somebody has to.

Write me back cuz I feel like I just told your ass too much.

Sincerely,

Quan

6

Disclose

This part should probably be a snapshot. That's definitely how it stands out in Quan's mind. *Snapshot: Two Dudes on the Roof of an Abandoned House—The End of the Beginning.*

He was maybe five months into the organization— and that's really what it was. An organization. There were meetings: one, Wednesday nights; one, Saturday mornings. There were rules: no underage drinking—which had been the catalyst for Trey's sobriety; no tobacco usage; no hard drugs: "'lean,' pills, and all that opioid trash included"; no "dumb shit," as Martel put it: theft (petty or grand), traffic violations, unnecessary fights, unprotected sex (*"Some li'l girl come up in here telling me one of y'all got her pregnant, it's gone be hell to pay."*).

Then there was business. And contrary to popular assumption, Martel Montgomery was not a drug dealer.

He sold weaponry.

Arms.

Quan started out on security detail like all the new recruits. But when it emerged that he was a bit of a math whiz, his assignments shifted (*way* quicker than he knew was typical) to counting money. Making sure the right amount had been paid, and then separating each person's cut and stuffing envelopes for distribution to the crew members.

And everyone took an instant liking to Quan, largely because he was good with numbers and suggested a minor tweak to the sales model that increased profit by seven percent.

After a group ass-whuppin' that left him with a black eye, sprained wrist, and bruised ribs (I tripped and fell down the stairs, he'd told his probation officer. Always worked for Mama, so . . .), Quan had been lovingly welcomed into the fold.

He still more or less kept to himself, though.

Looking back, for the life of him, Quan can't figure out what possessed him to be so . . .

open

with Trey the night the two boys wound up on the roof of an abandoned house. Yeah, Dwight had come in drunk and gone on a rampage. Yeah, while Dwight had been yelling and throwing shit and making ridiculous accusations about Mama and "conjugal visits" to Daddy, Quan had secreted Dasia and Gabe away to the hiding place Dwight was never lucid enough to think of (dumbass). Yeah, Dwight had threatened Quan and Quan'd had to flash the .22 cal he always wanted to use but knew he couldn't.

But none of that had been new.

In fact, that *exact* scenario had happened three times in the five months since Quan joined the Black Jihad. And every time before, he'd just . . . left. Sometimes he'd take a walk to cool off. Clear his head.

By the time he got back home, Dwight would either be passed out or gone. (Quan did find him crying his eyes out at the kitchen table once, but he tries not to think about Dwight being *human*. Too confusing.)

Other times he'd swing by Martel's to see if he had anything for Quan to do, or he'd go to Brad's or DeMarcus's to "shoot the shit" and watch movies or play video games.

But outside of that first-ever conversation Quan'd had with Martel, he never really talked about his problems at home.

Why this night was different, Quan still isn't sure. Maybe it was because he changed his mind en route to Brad's and took a right at the top of the hill instead of a left. Maybe it was because as he approached the end of this new-to-him street, he saw a couple.

He watched as the guy gently took the girl's hand and pulled her into a loving embrace.

And they rocked. Side to side.

Then they unstuck their upper bodies from each other . . .
and kissed.

Quan felt like a creep, but he couldn't pull his eyes away. Other than in movies, he'd never seen anything like it.

Maybe it was because as the couple broke apart, the guy caught sight of Quan (*staring*) and called his name.

It was Trey.

And Trey could *always* tell when something was . . . off.

Not just with Quan.

With anyone.

Dude had a

sixth

sense.

(Shit was eerie.)

Trey did his *all-seeing eye* thing—looking at Quan head to toe, Trey's brow pulling down in the process—and said,

Trin, I'll see you later, okay, babe?

before watching the girl head up the walkway

to the house.

Then he turned to Quan and said,

Ey, come on with me, bruh.

(Quan complied, as usual.)

They took a few more turns and wound up at a house that looked like it hadn't been lived in for years. Quan followed Trey around the back, up onto a back porch that looked ready to crumble, and inside through a sliding glass door.

It was dark inside but

maybe seeing

     the mattress

       and duffel bag

         in the corner

           of an empty room

             and coming to realize

this was probably where Trey slept—

     lived—

made Quan a little more emotional than he typically allowed himself to get.

Maybe that's why when they got to the roof and Trey pulled out his trusty vape pen (which was dying . . . because the house didn't have electricity, Quan realized. What would Trey do when winter came? It didn't get *that* cold in Georgia, but there were nights here and there . . .) and asked Quan what was up, Quan

                    SPILLED.

Four days later—a Tuesday—Quan got called to the front office at school.

   His heart

             beat

  in his

  throat

    ears

     skull

the whole way out the door

       down the stairs

         and up the hall

from English class.

He racked his brain trying to figure out what he'd done and how bad it would be.

He'd missed curfew a few times . . . had he been reported? Mama was always threatening to call his probation officer . . . had she done it? Had someone, somehow found out about the vape cartridge he'd forgotten was in his pocket and accidentally brought on campus? (Not that he even used the thing . . . random piss tests were no joke.)

How much trouble was this gonna get him in with Martel?

By the time he got to the office he was mentally preparing for what he was going to *say* to Tel—if he even got the opportunity to talk to him before they carted his ass back to detention for violating his probation.

So lost in these preparations was Quan, when he walked in and saw his mama, he literally stumbled backward.

Especially since she was

       crying.

The principal—a black dude in his early thirties that Quan wasn't too familiar with, so intent was he on staying *out* of trouble—offered a box of tissues to Mama. She snatched a few and blew her nose.

Quan couldn't come up with a single thing to say, so the

densest silence he'd ever felt coated the air, making it hard to breathe.

It dragged.

Thickened.

The principal (uncomfortably) cleared his throat.

Quan gulped.

"Mama?"

Then she met his eyes.

Her chin got to quivering and she stood

and threw herself onto Quan.

It took him a second to catch on and wrap his arms around her—it'd been so long since she'd hugged him.

As he did, all the fight went out of her. An exhale of respite soaked in a deluge of trembling grief.

That's when Quan knew.

"Dwight . . ."

He knew. *Man*, did he know. In that instant, Quan knew more than he'd ever be able to disclose.

So he shut his eyes. Waited for the bomb she was dropping to hit the floor and blow up every bit of ground he currently stood on.

He could swear he felt the **BOOM** when it did.

"Dwight's dead."

Snapshot:

A Boy Alone on
a Run-Down
Playground
(2017)

The rocket ship is gone.

Which Quan knew in theory: he heard somebody OD'd inside it and was discovered by a kid young enough to believe the guy was sleeping.

But seeing the empty space where it used to be—especially right *now* when he needs a place of refuge more than anything else in the world—makes him feel like a similar hole has opened up inside him.

Well . . . another one. The Dad-hole was already there. So was the *youthful innocence* one. ("There's a hole inside me where my childhood should've been," he told Martel once.)

This hole feels like an ending. A door: closed, triple deadbolted and then welded shut. No going back through it. No returning to the other side. The rope to Quan's final sliver of hope for a brighter future, for the fulfillment of some inner potential he didn't realize he still believed in—for a way UP and out . . .

Gone.

Just like his way into imaginary outer space.

It's not even the fact that duck-ass, Olaf-ass Dwight is gone. About *that*, Quan couldn't be more relieved. Which he does feel a little weird about: being . . . happy. Thankful even. That a person is dead.

(Quan's never been more thankful in his life for *that*.)

He drops down onto a graffiti-covered bench and looks around. Remembering. When life was—seemed—simpler. When he used to come here to actually *play*. When the rubber ground didn't have pockmarks and the spiral slide didn't have cusswords carved into the side. He recalls the night he met Justyce McAllister—who now goes to some white school on the rich side of town.

When was the last time Justyce came home? Does dude even consider Wynwood Heights *home* anymore?

Did he ever? It's not like he really fit in . . . What would Justyce say if he saw that the rocket was gone?

Quan looks at the broken swing. Another way to fly, rendered useless.

But Justyce got out. Justyce took off. Has Justyce become like Quan's salmon-on-the-river-eating cousin? (Who Quan hasn't seen or spoken to since. #family)

Quan's gaze drops. Lands on a word carved into one of the bench's wooden slats in little-kid lettering:

F U K C

What are kids like *Quan* supposed to do?

He swipes at his dampening eyes and shifts them back to the black hole where his galactic getaway vehicle used to be.

Dwight is dead.

And Quan is here. Stuck. Grounded.

Forever.

No getting out.

No flying away.

No lifting off.

Because Dwight's death wasn't an accident.

It was arranged.

Mama doesn't know it, of course. But Quan does.

Before Quan came looking for his rocket, he'd left his grieving mother and siblings—*half*-siblings . . . who no longer have a dad—and he'd gone to Martel's.

As soon as Quan was seated, Martel said, "Your mama okay?"

"Nah, man. Not really" was Quan's response.

Martel nodded. "She will be."

Silence.

And then: "I wish you woulda told me, Vernell."

"Huh?"

"You heard me," Martel said. "You shoulda told me how bad it was. How am I supposed to help you if you don't tell me things?"

HELP me? Quan thought.

"Nobody should have to live the way y'all were livin', man. Especially not one of *my* guys."

At this, Quan dropped his chin. Hearing himself referenced in such a way caused quite the unexpected surge of emotion.

Martel wasn't done, though.

"Here."

And he held out an envelope to Quan. Who peeked inside.

It was full of money.

"Give that to your moms. Should hold her over for a few months. Hopefully by then she'll have healed up and found some work. Just tell her some community members heard about y'all's loss and wanted to help out."

Quan didn't say a word. Couldn't.

"Next time you got a problem, I need to hear about it from *you*, not Montrey. You hear me?"

Quan nodded.

"Ey, look at me."

Quan did. Though he wished he could look away.

"The safety of our members and their families is one of the highest priorities of this organization. Any person or thing threatening that safety will be swiftly taken care of," Martel said, steel in his eyes, his voice, the set of his shoulders. "You got me?"

Quan nodded again without breaking eye contact. "Yes, sir."

"Now get on outta here. I'm sure your mama could use her baby boy at home tonight."

And Quan stood and walked to the door.

Numb.

Just as his hand wrapped around the knob, Martel spoke again from behind him: "Hey, Vernell . . ."

Quan looked over his shoulder.

Martel was staring at him, eagle-eyed. "You don't have nothin' else to say?"

"Huh?"

Martel just stared. And stared. And just as Quan started to feel like there were spiders crawling beneath his skin, he caught on. His gaze dropped, but he forced it back up.

Gulped. Drug the words together and shoved them off his tongue: "Thank you."

Martel smiled. "That's better. See you tomorrow at Morning Meeting?"

An order cloaked as a question. Met with a single nod. "Yes, sir."

"Excellent. You be good, all right? All shall be well." And Martel turned and disappeared back into the living room.

It all feels like a joke now. *Be good.*

He's *been* good since he got out. He's done all he's supposed to. Stays out of trouble. No drugs or alcohol or skipping school or letting his grades slip.

That other kind of good, though? As Quan looks around, he *knows* that his life has gone the way of this playground: once bright and bouncy and filled with ways to take flight (both real and imaginary), now beat down and broken. Hopeless.

Now there's nowhere to run to. No places to hide.
Quan looks down at the misspelled cussword again.
That's how he feels.

FUKCed

Because his rocket ship is gone.
His escape is gone.
Now there's no way out.

7

Disaster

It was supposed to be a quick drop. In fact, Quan was *determined* to make it quick because he had something important to get back to: while cleaning out the front closet, Mama found a box full of crap that belonged to Dwight.

Inside was a beat-up shoebox.

Inside the shoebox was a stack of manila envelopes.

Inside the manila envelopes . . .

were letters.

From Daddy.

Like over a hundred of them.

For a while, Daddy had written once a week. Then once every two weeks. Then down to once a month.

The first letter was sent in April 2012: four months post-arrest, and just after he'd been sentenced and moved to the maximum-security facility in Reidsville, Georgia.

Final one was postmarked September 27, 2016.

Fo(u)r *YEARS* Daddy wrote to Quan. Consistently.

And duck-ass, Count Olaf-ass Dwight *hid* his letters. (May his wack-ass, devil-ass soul toil eternally in turmoil. And snakes.)

He'll never admit it to anybody, but he cried as he read the first one.

Anyway, the plan was to:

1. Complete his very simple assignment, which involved—
   a. At the predetermined time, picking up the black leather, payment-filled pouch the Black Jihad's biggest client left where he always left it: in the mailbox of a house Martel owned. (Turns out he also owned the one Trey slept in when not at his girl's house. Martel owned quite a few houses in the neighborhood.)
   b. Counting the contents, and
   c. Delivering said pouch to Martel's.

Again: simple.

Then once he was done, he planned to:

2. Head straight home to continue reading his letters, taking notes so he could respond in a way that would let Daddy know he'd read every.
   a. single.
   b. one.

Which felt a little bit corny, but whatever: the realization that Daddy had tried to stay in contact made Quan feel like . . . well, he couldn't even put it into words.

The pickup and cash-counting proceeded as planned. Which was a relief. Quan held his breath with every bill that passed through his fingertips, low-key expecting one to be missing—looking back, that was a common thing for him: presuming *something* would go wrong at the times he really needed *everything* to happen without incident.

But it was all there.

It was the delivery that went south.

Martel was having a birthday party. About a month prior, he'd gotten pulled over in Alabama, and since crossing a state line is a probation violation, he'd been sentenced to twelve months of house arrest. So he brought the party to him.

It'd been going on for maybe an hour and a half when Quan arrived. The music was loud (where it was coming from, he couldn't tell), and there were people everywhere the eye could see: front lawn, porch, driveway. Quan had to do a good bit of bobbing and weaving to reach the front door.

Everything was cool at first. Martel saw Quan come in and summoned him over to where he was kicked back in a *new* round bamboo-framed chair with a giant cushion that looked like it was wrapped in dashiki material. Quan even pulled the envelope from the kangaroo pouch of his hoodie as he moved through the room—it was quieter and there were fewer people *inside* the house, thank goodness—so he could just hand it over and bounce.

But Martel had clearly had a beverage or two (it *was* his birthday). And was chatty.

"Well, if it isn't my favorite bookkeeper!" he crowed as Quan approached. "I take it everything was in order?"

Quan nodded and passed him the package. "Yep."

"And how are *you*? Everything cool?"

More nodding. "Everything is definitely cool."

"Hey, speaking of 'cool,' peep my new papasan chair!" Martel ran his hands lovingly along the edge of the massive kente cloth seat.

Quan smiled for real. It was odd seeing Martel so geeked about something so simple. "It's dope, Tel."

"How's your moms? She good?"

Quan really wanted to go. He shoved his hands in his pockets and rocked back on his heels. "She's great!"

"You sure you good?" And Martel's expression shifted just the smallest bit. Like some of the joy leached out. "Seem like you in a hurry—"

Which was when Brad burst into the room. Grill on his lower teeth gleaming, blond hair tied up in a funny-looking baby bun on top of his head. "Ey yo, Tel, twelve just rolled by."

Quan's whole body went dry-ice cold. If the cops "rolled by," there was a good chance they'd return. What with the music blasting and who knows how many people *loitering* around the house, Quan was sure they were in violation of some obscure ordinance no one would know existed until they were slapped with random-ass charges.

He tried to keep his breathing under control. Since Dwight's demise, Quan had been having these . . . spells. Where it would suddenly get real hard to take a breath and he'd be absolutely, positively, 140 percent sure horrible things were about to happen. Like the cops would bust in and snatch him up the way they'd taken Daddy all those years ago. They would pin Dwight's murder on Quan and hit him with the death penalty without him even going to trial.

His eyes darted around looking for the easiest escape.

Martel's eyes narrowed. "People started dispersing already?"

"Yeah." Brad rapid-fire nodded and his boy-bun bobbed. Quan almost laughed.

Almost.

"Good," Martel said. "Tell a few of our guys to come inside, and you and Montrey find DeMarcus and post up by the truck. If they come back, chances are they'll block the driveway."

Brad nodded—just once this time. "Cool."

"Vernell, you go with Bradley."

"Huh?" The word (*is* that even a word?) was out of Quan's mouth before he could catch it.

And if looks could truly **shoot daggers,** as Quan's read in a few books, he woulda been a whole shish kabob.

115

"We really need to eliminate that from your vocabulary, Vernell."

"Sorry, sorry," Quan said, kicking into gear and rushing after Brad.

With each step, the ball of dread that'd formed in Quan's lower gut the moment he heard *twelve* (he legit had gas now) expanded and expanded, and by the time he and Brad reached Trey and a couple of the others at Martel's Range Rover in the driveway, Quan could swear he had developed a headache, heartburn, the runs, and charley horses in both legs.

Something bad was about to happen. He could tell.

Brad delivered Martel's message to Trey, who then dispatched a few other guys to clear the stragglers in the front yard. Some left, some headed to the back.

Trey then popped the rear hatch of the truck and sat in the trunk space, letting his legs dangle over the edge. "Brad, take left flank. Quan, you got right. Mar, you post up next to me."

Mar. As in DeMarcus Johnson, Quan's former classmate who'd gotten expelled in middle school because he couldn't get a grip on his rage. He'd joined up with Black Jihad four months prior, and now Quan *knew* knew something bad was about to go down. Mar treated his pistol like he did clean underwear: never left home without it on him.

Even now, Quan could see him shifting it around in his waistband. Something Quan knew now that he didn't know in middle school: Mar's dad had been shot and killed by a police officer during a traffic stop gone wrong . . . and he'd been in the car.

>*"He TOLD dude he was carrying and had a license to do so. Heard that shit with my own ears, dawg. Then he said OUT LOUD that he was gonna get his wallet out his pocket. He SAID it. Cop pulled the trigger soon as Pops reached. I'll NEVER forget that shit."*

(That's when Mar's face would go granite-hard and he would absentmindedly feel for the butt of the piece that lived just inside the rim of his belted pants.)

> (That officer was indicted and tried, but acquitted.)

>> (Because of the "anger problem" Mar displayed in school—

after the incident—

he was deemed not competent to testify.)

Trey also checked for *his* weapon.

Which made Quan's ankle itch. Because *Quan's* little .22 was tucked in his sock. He only had it because he'd had to make that damn pickup.

"There they go," Mar said as the nose of the cruiser appeared at the corner.

"I told yo ass they was comin' back," Trey said to Brad. "Now gimme my money."

Brad reached into his pocket, and a slip of green was slapped into Trey's palm. "Damn!" Brad said.

The police cruiser hung a right and crept up the street toward them.

"Y'all get in position," Trey said.

Quan's heart beat faster. Almost like an internal drumroll that would lead to a mind-shattering *BANG* of cymbals.

Just like Tel said, the cruiser pulled right across the edge of the driveway

and stopped.

(Which meant they were parked in the direction of oncoming traffic. Bold.)

Then the doors opened. And two officers got out.

And Quan's consciousness detached from his body. Or something. All he knows is it suddenly felt like he was watching a movie:

THE END
a short film

Starring:

Officer Garrett Tison—White, salt-and-pepper gray hair, middle-aged and paunchy, looks a couple shakes past "ready to retire"

Officer Tomás "Tommy" Castillo—looks white, early thirties, military buzz cut, buff and puffed up and ready to fight some crime

Montrey David Filly—African American, eighteen, long and lean with shoulder-length locs and very little impulse control

Bradley Craig Mathers—White, seventeen, blond boy-bun, gold grill that spells BRAD across his lower teeth

Martel Montgomery—African American, thirty, tall with an athletic build and faded haircut, cool/confident exterior

Vernell LaQuan Banks Jr.—African American, sixteen, bystander(ish)

Setting:

EXTERIOR: Martel Montgomery's driveway and front yard—nighttime

After exiting their car, the two officers, with hands on their utility belts near their firearms, approach the group of boys gathered in the driveway around an older-model luxury SUV.

> TISON

Evening, fellas.

> TREY

'Sup, officers?

> TISON

Sorry to disrupt your night, but
we received a complaint about the
noise level.

> BRAD

Lemme guess: Barbie and Ken up
the road called cuz they didn't
get an invite to the cookout.

All the boys laugh. Castillo instinctively
grips the handle of his holstered gun.

> BRAD (CONT'D)
> (raising his hands)

Whoa now, officer. It was a joke.

> TREY
> (to the other boys)

One of y'all let Martel know the
cops are here.

Quan jogs up to the house—uncomfortably
thanks to the small firearm rubbing against
his bare ankle—and disappears inside.
Castillo, with his hand still on his gun,
sizes each boy up.

A few people leave the house and head away on
foot before MARTEL MONTGOMERY comes out onto
the porch, hands in pockets, with a small
group of African American boys behind him.

Quan returns to the group at the SUV.
(Though he has no idea why and doesn't
remember the walk.)

                    MARTEL
          (shouting)
     Something I can help you with,
     officers?

                    TISON
     Need ya to keep your hands where
     I can see 'em, son.

Martel smirks, pulls his hands out, and
raises them.

                    MARTEL
     My apologies.

                    121

                    TISON

You're the owner of this home?

                    MARTEL

That I am.

                    TISON

You, uhh . . .

(beat as he looks around)

    . . . mind if we have a word?

                    MARTEL

Sure, but—

Martel grabs the right side of his pants,
and Tison freezes, hand hovering near his
firearm. Behind him, Castillo shifts into
a shooting stance, gun drawn and aimed at
Martel, who lifts his pant leg, revealing
his ankle monitor.

              MARTEL (CONT'D)

—can't leave the porch.

Tison exhales and relaxes.

                    TISON

All right, we're coming to you.

MARTEL

That's cool. But I'd appreciate
your partner lowering his weapon
before approaching my house.

Tison's head whips around.

TISON
(under his breath)
Put your goddamn gun down!

CASTILLO

You sure you trust these assholes?

TISON

Whether or not I trust 'em is
irrelevant, kid. There are
twelve of them and two of us.
Lower it.

CASTILLO

No disrespect, sir, but I'm not
sure that's a good idea.

TISON
(to Martel)
Bear with us a moment, please.

Martel nods once and crosses his arms.

Quan definitely isn't breathing. The itch
at his ankle becomes a burn as his eyes
trace the barrel of Castillo's pistol to
its target: the one man who's actually been
around and worked to keep Quan safe and on
some semblance of a straight and narrow.

Quan tugs at his own pant leg without
thinking.

                    TISON (CONT'D)
               (coaxing, to Castillo)
          Tommy, I know you're scared, but
          you gotta lower the weapon before
          things escalate.

                    CASTILLO
          I'm sorry, sir, but I can't do
          that. I know what guys like these
          are capable of—

There's sudden movement beside the Range
Rover, and Castillo whips right with his
gun still extended.

               BANG
               BANG

(ducking)

The fu—

BANG

CUT TO BLACK

Quan blinked.

There was ringing in his ears. Then shouting. And cussing.

Blinked.

Somebody bumped his arms, which he realized were extended in front of him.

Blinked.

His head swam and there was a sharp twinge in his temple as the ringing died away and the blinding, spinning light of the police cruiser came into focus.

When had that been turned on?

"Dawg, we gotta MOVE!" someone said, grabbing him by the upper arm and pulling **hard.**

That's when Quan noticed the body on the ground. Facedown. Dressed in all blue. Military buzz cut. Buff.

But no longer puffed up.

There was a dark spot expanding in the grass beneath his upper half.

"Quan, let's GO!"

That's when Quan noticed the gun in his hand.

And dropped it.

Then he allowed himself to be pulled into a

run.

September 10, 2017

Dear Dad,

　　I don't really even know how to start this letter. I've tried five times now, and can't seem to find the right words.

　　Part of the problem is there's too much to write. A lot has happened since that night they took you away, and to catch you up on everything would take time I'm not really sure I have at this point.

　　I will say: I got YOUR letters . . . all 104 of them. I read every single one, and now I owe you an apology. Maybe that's the best place to start . . .

　　I'm sorry, Dad. For not writing you sooner. Not that I could've responded to the letters you sent ME—for reasons wholly outside my control, I only gained access to them a few days ago, almost a full year after you stopped writing. But even that is saying something, isn't it? Whether I knew about it or not, you wrote to me consistently for over four years without ever receiving a response.

　　I could've done the same.

　　I also want to apologize for letting myself believe you'd given up on me. When I got to some of the later letters you wrote and realized you've been under the impression I'D given up on YOU . . . I dunno. It kinda stabbed me in the heart a little bit.

Imma be real, Dad: I've never really felt like I've had much . . . power, I guess. But reading that last letter from you . . . That one part where you say you know you made some mistakes and you wouldn't blame me for "wanting to pretend (you) don't exist," but that you hope I never forget that you love me "and will always want only the best" for me . . . Man. That really made me feel some type of way.

I didn't realize I could make YOU feel like that, Dad. It seems so backwards. You're the parent and I'm the kid. I guess I just assumed my feelings toward you didn't really matter because you're the one with the authority? I don't know how to explain it.

Let me make it clear (even though I feel kinda funny writing it): Dad, I could NEVER forget you and I have NEVER wanted to pretend like you don't exist. And I'm sorry for EVER making you feel like I could.

Everything is just real messed up. Everything.

Which leads me to my final apology: I failed, Dad. I failed to become what you believed I could be. I've gotten in a lot of trouble over the years, and I'm in some trouble now.

It's too much to explain right now, but after you got taken away, bad thing after bad thing after bad thing started happening. Your letters were hidden from me for a long time because of some of those bad things. And the person who hid them is no longer with us (which is another kinda-bad thing that might've led to a definitely bad thing).

Anyway, without you, I didn't really have anybody in my corner. I'm sure that sounds like an excuse, but it's true. Mama had her own stuff going on, and my favorite teacher left, and it seemed like no matter how good I TRIED to do, it never worked. And I really did try. I need you to believe me on that.

I don't want to think too much about it because there's nothing that can be done about it now, and that makes me real mad . . . but I can't help but wonder how different things might've been if I'd gotten your letters when you sent them. Honestly, I just cried as I read your words about how much you believed in me and how you were taking responsibility for your actions, but you knew I was headed in a different direction. How "thinking about all the great things" I would do is what kept you going.

Dad, if I'd known that, I would've . . . I dunno. Maybe I would've . . .

I can't even write it.

Doesn't matter now. I chose my path. Though, real talk—and I promise this isn't me making an excuse—I don't really see where there was a different path for a dude like me. Just like there probably wasn't a different one for a dude like you. Is what it is, right?

I'm likely going away for a long time, but I wouldn't have

129

been able to live with myself if I didn't let you know I love you and I'll never give up on you, Dad. There's this part of me that feels like I'm supposed to be mad at you for being gone, but . . . I'm not. Especially not now, knowing you were writing to me all those years.

I just wanna say thank you. For your words. Even though I didn't know about them until it was too late.

Actually, I take that back. It's not too late. Your letters reminded me of my power, and now I know what I gotta do.

I love you, Dad. Stay up, aiight?

One day we'll meet again. I hope.

Your son,

Jr.

April 24

Dear Justyce,

    Man, your ass had a LOTTA questions in that last letter you sent. What's crazy is Doc and Liberty (She so damn fine, bruh. I'm not a religious fella, but good LAWD.) have been asking me some of the same shit . . . which means I actually have some answers.

    Before we get into all THAT, though, I have news: your boy is three and a half weeks away from becoming a high school graduate. I get to put on a cap and gown and the whole nine (over my jumpsuit, but still).

    I'm getting a little emotional thinking about it. Like I'm excited . . . but I'm also mad. Even sad.

    Weird seeing me write that, ain't it? A dude is up in here gettin' in touch with his feelings and shit. I was extra tired a few weeks ago, and slipped up and told Doc about these episodes I have sometimes. He said something to somebody around here, and next thing I know, I'd been assigned to a new counselor. Black lady named Tay—short for Octavia, but she said don't call her that (I feel it). She's got this blond fade that makes me wish I could hit the barbershop, and she's probably the coolest adult female I've ever met—though I'll

131

admit it took me a minute to warm up to her. WAY easier to talk to than Agnes, the overly chipper middle-aged white woman they had me with before. I pretty much NEVER talked to her out-of-touch ass.

Getting back to the point: Tay said she's pretty sure I've been having "panic attacks" (which sounds mad violent, don't it?) and I have that same PTSD thing I remember you saying your dad dealt with. I thought it was only linked to being in the military and going to war, but apparently a lot of the stuff I went through as a kid qualifies as "trauma" and my brain has created these . . . reactions to anything that reminds me of the traumatic events. She calls them "triggers"—which IS a trigger (the psychological kind she be talking about), so I've been referring to them as sparks.

And writing about them.

A lot of my current sparks are linked to the night you asked about (though I definitely have some that are MAD old . . . like going back to when my dad was arrested). And the more I think and talk about it, the more frustrated I get. Like Doc pushes my ass HARD in these academics. And it's kind of a weird thing, but him believing I COULD "write a compelling argumentative essay that either supports or refutes the continued use of Harper Lee's To Kill a Mockingbird as a seminal text on American racism" (THIS guy) made me want to prove him right.

And THEN, every time I DO prove him right, and he hands me something with a "Fantastic job!" scrawled across the top

(Bruh, how did you even read this dude's handwriting??), I feel good for like five minutes . . .

But then the buzzer will sound to let a guard in or out, or a cell door will close, or I'll suddenly notice all the iron and concrete. And where I am—where I'm likely gonna BE for a long-ass time—will hit me. Hard.

I guess I didn't realize just how big of a difference it could make to have somebody really believe in you. I been thinking a lot about Trey and Mar and Brad and them. We were all looking for the same things, man—support, protection, family, that type of shit. And we found SOME of it in one another, but we couldn't really give each other no type of encouragement to do nothing GOOD because nobody was really giving US any. Matter fact, we typically got the opposite. People telling us how "bad" we were. Constantly looking at us like they expected only the worst.

How the hell's a person supposed to give something they ain't never had?

Do I wish I woulda had more people to point out the good in me after my dad got taken away? That WE, every single dude in my crew, had had that? Yeah. Prolly wouldn't be sittin' here in (cell)block three, spilling all my guts out to you in this letter.

There's a good chance that if we'd had the kinda support you had—dudes like Doc, for instance, who told us we could really do and be something, and who believed it—none of us woulda been at Tel's that night.

133

Which brings me to your main question: What actually happened the night Tomás Castillo got popped?

Well, to be honest with you, a lot of the details are lost. When I try to REMEMBER remember, which is something Tay is always tryna get me to do, I have these like vivid flashes blended in with stretches of black.

That prolly don't even make sense to your hyper-logical, ivy-leaguing ass.

What I will say: despite my sorta-off memory of what happened that night, there are two things I can tell you for SURE:

Number one: under ANY other circumstances, the whole thing would've been considered self-defense. Castillo not only had his gun out, he had it aimed. When I was reading that one letter from you where you told me the details of your encounter with him, I was shaking my head the whole time because that was definitely the same shit we were dealing with. He walked up SO certain things were gonna go south, he basically forced them in that direction, you feel me?

In one of my flashes, he's got his gun pointed at Martel. I couldn't really hear much because there was this roaring in my ears like I was standing next to a jet. Fight or flight on infinity. I don't remember pulling my weapon, but next thing I knew, Castillo's 9mm Glock was swinging toward US.

Now according to GA Code O.C.G.A. Sec. 16-3-21(a)— you best believe I looked that shit up and memorized it—"A person is justified in threatening or using force against another when and to the extent that he or she reasonably believes that such threat or force is necessary to defend himself or herself or a third person against such other's imminent use of unlawful force."

The fact that a cop was involved complicates things, obviously, and my lawyer doesn't think we'll get very far with the claim "considering the backgrounds of the young men we'd be calling as witnesses." (His exact words. Which is exactly the shit I was talking about, but whatever.)

But you best believe I intend to use that shit in court. What I CAN do is stand by my own damn principles. Nobody can take THAT from me. Things went the way they went, and I made the decision I made. I know that because there was a police officer involved and I have a record, this case might as well be closed.

I'm not going down without at least a little bit of a fight, though. Because this is the second thing I know for sure: I'm not the only one who pulled a gun that night. In fact, there wasn't only one, but THREE others who did.

Yes, I felt like I owed a debt because of some stuff that was done to ensure the safety and well-being of my family. So I wound up taking the charge. (That interrogation was the worst thing I've ever experienced, by the way. Never wanna go through anything like it ever again.)

I think I told you before that Doc once asked me if I was a killer. Back then, I couldn't really answer, but now I can.

So. I want YOU to know—even though nobody else outside my immediate circle ever will (right?): the answer is no.

I'm not a killer.

I pulled my gun, but I never actually fired.

I'm not the one who killed Tomás Castillo.

—Q

PART TWO

Just Beginning

Snapshot:

A Postscript
(Present Day)

P.S.:

I'm not gonna tell you who did it.
So don't even ask.

Snapshot:

Two Boys
and a Girl in a Car
(Present Day)

Justyce McAllister has a lot on his mind during the almost thirteen-hour drive from New York back to Georgia.

Finals, obviously. He *thinks* he did pretty good on everything—though that last "short answer" question on the ethics exam was suspect. He *knows* he did better than Rosie the Racist Roommate on the Calc II final: dude tossed his paper at the professor as he left the classroom, and was still fuming about "that utter bullshit Calc II exam" as he packed to leave yesterday.

That's another thing: while Jus certainly wasn't sad to see Roosevelt Carothers's back as he walked out of their shared space for the last time, it was weird to realize there's a chance he'll never see the dude again.

Oddly enough, Justyce has come to pity his roommate just the slightest bit. Yeah, Roosevelt comes from hella money and more or less has the whole world at his fingertips, but homie is the furthest thing from happy Justyce has ever seen. It's occurred to Justyce how pointless it is to have access to basically everything when you're a person who's satisfied by nothing. The more time Jus has spent around the guy, the more he's realized just how sad and pitiful dude's life actually is.

Justyce's life, though, is rich and full. He joined the BSAY (aka Black Student Alliance at Yale) and was one of eight freshmen selected to the newest class of the Yale Debate Association. He found his people, his grades are solid, and his long-distance relationship with the world's finest Jewish girl has been working out just . . . well, fine.

It's baffling, Jus thinks as the trees blur by near the state line between the two Carolinas. His first Yale year is over, and he made it through with very little personal turmoil to write home about.

And write home, Justyce did. Not to his mama—there was a phone for all that—but to Quan Banks.

Childhood playmate. (*1 . . . 2 . . . 3 . . . BLAST OFF!*)

Fellow smart guy. (Though Quan didn't seem to want anybody to know it.)

Cousin of Justyce's slain best friend.

Rich and restless Roosevelt's polar opposite.

On a hunch, Jus decided to check his PO box one last time before leaving campus, and he found a letter that must've gotten lost in the mail for a minute: it'd been postmarked more than two weeks prior.

And what was in that letter?

Still has Jus shook.

There's movement behind him in the back seat. Then a groan. And an overly loud yawn. "Are we there yet?"

"Eww, why is it talking?" comes a groggy second voice from the passenger seat. This one makes Jus smile. And shake his head.

"Aww, SJ! I'm super thrilled to be with you too!"

Jared Christensen puts a hand on Sarah-Jane Friedman's shoulder—then quickly snatches it back when she thumps the crap out of it. "Oww! Jesus!"

"No touchy."

"Ahh, come on, pal! Can't we bury the hatchet? It's not like you can get away from me now. I'm sure J-Man told you we're rooming together next year—"

"A decision I'm still questioning." She hits Justyce with the kind of side-eye that could slice glass.

He'd never tell her, but he kinda loves it when she looks at him like that. "Ah, he's not so bad, babe." Jus winks and takes her hand.

"Exactly!" from Jared. "I'm a changed man!"

"Changed man, my ass," SJ says, pulling away from Justyce. She crosses her arms and looks out the window. "I still can't believe you agreed to let that douchenozzle ride home with us."

"I'm literally right here behind you—"

"Yeah, well, you shouldn't be. *My* boyfriend shouldn't be bearing the burden of responsibility of getting you home safely."

"'Burden of responsibility' feels a *tad* strongly worded—"

"Well, that's exactly what it is. We all know who Daddy Christensen would go after if something happened to you on this ride."

"Babe, *relax*," Justyce says, more an attempt to cut through the tension in the car than anything.

Because . . . well, she's right. It's not like Justyce doesn't KNOW that. Jared surely knows it too because he doesn't try to deny it.

And now something Jus has been trying to keep *off* his mind crawls right to the front of it: his newfound friendship with Jared Christensen.

True to his word, after their chance encounter at the grave site of their mutual best friend Manny Rivers, Jus did reach out to Jared once they returned to school.

And much to SJ's chagrin, the two have been thick as thieves ever since. Honestly, having a little piece of home around has been helpful for Jus considering the two people he cares most about—Mama and SJ—are people he doesn't get to see as often as he'd like. And while Jared definitely still has a ways to go, he is doing better. In fact, if Jus had a dollar for every time dude said *"Bro, lemme know if I need a privilege check on this, but . . ."* Jus could probably cover next semester's tuition.

Jus peeps at Jared in the rearview—he's staring out the window with his jaw clenched—and then down at his own arm, where the face of an heirloom watch meant to go to that friend he and Jared both lost stares up at him. Jus can't help but think Manny would be happy to see the Justyce/Jared beef squashed, grilled in one of those Big Green Egg things white people seem to be partial to, and served medium-well.

"You're enabling him, Justyce," SJ continues, snatching him back.

"*Enabling* me?" from Jared.

SJ whips around, so pissed, Jus is tempted to roll all the windows down so her fury can fly free. "Yes, asshole," she snaps. "Let's unpack things, shall we? Why are you here?"

"Huh?"

"*Here.* In THIS car instead of your own?"

Jared doesn't respond.

"Correct. Your license is suspended. Why?"

"Come on, S—"

"Can it, Jus. I get that you two are cool now, but him being here with us is very much not."

"Look, it's J-Man's car. He can drive whoever he wants—"

"Stop calling him that!" SJ rages. "His name is *Justyce*, and the fact that he's carting your ass home after YOU screwed up is a tragic miscarriage of the concept he's named for!"

"SJ, I *offered* him a ride," Justyce says. "You make it sound like I was coerced or this is some kinda assignment."

Now she locks *Jus* in the laser beams of her wrath. "Clearly we *all* need a refresher: Jared Peter Christensen is *here* because he got a DUI. Which is bad enough on its own, but there's more to it, isn't there? Not only did he try to *run* from the cops." Now she looks back at Jared. "Didn't get very far, did ya, party boy? You were too drunk to effing stand." Eyes back on Justyce for the grand finale: "He had a bag of pot in his pocket!"

"Marijuana is decriminalized in Connecticut," Jared says.

"SO WHAT? IT'S STILL ILLEGAL!" (She's on a roll

now.) "*Especially* in tandem with underage drunk driving! If Justyce—or any other African American!—had done what you did, they'd be in *jail*. Hell, he might even be dead! But *you*? Did they even put you in cuffs?"

Silence from the back seat.

From the driver's seat too. Jus would be lying if he said he hasn't thought every single word coming out of SJ's mouth right now.

"Of course they didn't. You rode to the police station with your hands free, didn't you? I know you did."

Another glance in the rearview lets Jus know SJ's words are hitting Jared hard. What she doesn't know is Jared *has* thought about all the stuff she's saying. He broke down (sobbing like a big, pink-cheeked baby) to Justyce about it a few weeks ago.

"Papa Christensen shows up with your family attorney, and *poof*: what should've been a felony charge results in nothing more than a slap on the wrist. You don't get to drive your little Beemer for a few months, big whoop." She shakes her head again and crosses her arms. "Wanna never suffer any real consequences? Straight-white-cis-maleness and money, friends. Keys to the goddamn kingdom."

"Quan didn't do it."

Jus has *no idea* what makes him say it out loud. In fact, now that it's out of his mouth, he's sure he wasn't supposed to tell anyone. *Especially* not his upper-middle-class Jewish girlfriend and a hella rich, hella white former denier of systemic racism. What the hell is Jus *doing*?

Too late now, though. They're both staring at him.

"Huh?" Jared says as SJ says, "What?"

"He's innocent."

"How do you know?" from SJ.

"He told me. In his latest letter." SJ and Jared both know about Quan's letters, though he's never really spoken of their contents. Until now, apparently.

"And you believe him?" Jared asks.

SJ turns *fully* around now. Jus can't see her face, but whatever expression she's wearing makes Jared literally put his hands up. "It's a legitimate question!"

"No it *isn't*, you entitled son of a bi—"

"I do believe him," Justyce says. "Wouldn't have brought it up if I didn't."

"See?" SJ rotates back forward. "Idiot."

"My apologies, Justyce. I wasn't thinking—"

"What else is new?" SJ grumbles.

They sit in a jittery silence for a minute before Jared says: "Forgive me if this next question is also rooted in privilege"—there's another dollar for Justyce—"but if Quan didn't do it, why is he in jail?"

Justyce: "It's complicated."

"Does he know who *did* do it?" Jared goes on.

Jus nods. "He does."

"Then why doesn't he just tell the cops?"

"Sweet lord, you are so obtuse," SJ says.

"Dudes like Quan don't snitch, man," from Justyce. He remembers Quan's first letter. How bothered he was by Jus dissociating himself from "those" black guys in Jus's own letters to Martin. "Dudes like *us*, I should say," Justyce corrects. "If I were in his position, I wouldn't snitch either."

Jus expects Jared to fire off another oblivious white dude question—"But like, I mean, why not?" would be fitting.

But Jared doesn't.

"So what do we do?" he says instead.

"Huh?"

"Like . . . to help him. All three of us are prelaw students at two of the most prestigious educational institutions in the world."

Neither Jus nor SJ responds. They do glance at each other in surprise, however.

"I mean, we *do* care about dismantling injustice, right? Should a young black man—a BOY, even!—who did *not* commit the crime be doing the time?"

Now Justyce smiles. He can't help it. "Couldn't've said it better myself, dawg," he says, taking his eyes off the road for a moment to smirk at SJ.

She huffs. "Fine. I swear to god, though, Jared, if this is an attempt to pad your resume, and you try to take credit—"

"You have my word that won't be the case," Jared says.

152

The silence that follows feels electrified. Charged with . . . hope.

It makes Justyce's fingertips tingle.

"So we doing this?" he says, meeting eyes with Jared in the rearview before kicking another look at SJ.

Jared's giant head appears between the front seats. "Whattya say, Sarah-Jane? Huh? You in?" He pokes her shoulder, and she swats his hand away.

"Could you be any more annoying?"

"He could," Jus says. "And so could I. You joining this mission or what?"

"Of course I am," she says.

"Yesssss!" Jared sticks a fist forward, and Justyce reaches out to bump it.

"Just do me a favor?" SJ continues to Justyce.

"Anything for you, baby girl."

She puts a palm against Jared's forehead and shoves him back into what Jus knows she would say is his proper place. "Keep your pet WASP away from me."

8

Deal

A single argumentative essay separates Quan from his high school diploma.

As such, he's sitting in the block study room across from Doc, brow furrowed. The only sound is his scratchy pencil, covering his lined white paper with the little graphite symbols that'll seal his fate.

"I love your assertion," Doc says. "And I agree: changing the rhetoric used when talking to and about African American youth *could* change their trajectories. But I need you to *expound*."

Quan grunts his assent.

In truth, he ain't in the best of moods. It's been three weeks and two days since he sent that letter to Justyce, confessing a thing that he's literally told **no one**.

Not that he hasn't been tempted to. Especially as of late. Matter fact, just yesterday Tay was explaining what happens to the brain when membership in a group or organization is achieved through mental or physical hardship ("*everlasting loyalty, often misplaced"*), and Quan almost spilled the beans then. He's been having nightmares again, this time about his own arrest. Not that said arrest was especially traumatic—cops showed up at Mama's house during dinner a few nights after the incident, and Quan didn't resist when they Mirandized and placed him under arrest—but the looks on Mama's and Gabe's faces (Dasia was at a friend's house, thank god) will likely haunt him forever.

Quan had known the police would come for him. From the moment he and Trey got to the house of Martel's Trey sometimes slept in, and Quan realized he no longer had his gun, he'd been 100 percent sure of where things were headed.

So he went home and read the rest of Daddy's letters. He wrote Daddy a letter of his own.

And then he

        waited

            for what

    he

        knew

        would eventually

            happen.

Then came the dilemma. Because while he would never snitch, the fact remained that he was being detained for a crime he didn't commit. He held his tongue for a while, but the more time he spent alone in that holding cell, the more his wheels spun. No, the ballistics of the bullets pulled from

Castillo's body wouldn't match those of Quan's firearm and they'd have to release him . . .

But then they'd start searching for the gun that *did* match. Which could lead to trouble for everyone, Martel especially. Quan knew what kind of contraband the guy had in his house. Which surely could lead to searches of Martel's *other* properties.

Quan couldn't let that happen. Especially not after everything Martel and the guys had done for him. He wouldn't've been able to live with himself.

Even still, the "confession" surprised Quan when it popped out of his mouth that day.

And just like that, his fate was signed, sealed, and delivered.

He didn't intend to tell Justyce the truth in that letter. It just . . . came out. On the paper. Like some poison pulled from his veins by the power of the pen.

And at first, he felt lighter, rubbing his thumb over the stamp to seal it to the envelope with Justyce's name and PO box address scrawled on it. Handing it over to be mailed felt like a pranayama exhale. (Tay taught him all about those during the deep-breathing exercises she was teaching him for his PTSD stuff.)

But over three weeks with no response?

Part of him felt ridiculous. In the grand scheme of things,

twenty-three days isn't *that* long. Doc did say Jus had finals last week and would be driving home from college . . . Maybe dude got held up studying or some shit.

But what if the letter got lost—or never got sent? Where would it be now? He hoped with everything in him that nobody *else* had read it.

Then again, what if Justyce read it and told somebody?

Quan's mind churns itself practically inside out at the thought of the cops running the ballistics and sending a search team to Martel's right this very minute.

He pauses to look down at his paper. Instead of his essay, what's written on the paper are the questions swirling in his head. He's losing it.

"Quan?" Doc says, startling him. "You all right over there?"

"Huh?"

"You look a little clammy. Listen, don't stress over this. You're going to do fine. I know it."

Quan drops his eyes and takes a deep breath.

Another one.

In for a five count through the nose

then out

just

as

slow.

Realign

his

prana.

(Or whatever.)

Then, "Doc, I gotta tell you somethi—"

The door to the classroom flies open, and the house-wide superintendent's frame fills the entryway. "Banks, you got a visitor."

Quan looks at Doc, who is clearly just as surprised (and why wouldn't he be?).

"Huh?" Quan says to the giant man eyeing Quan like he's waiting for him to strike.

"That was English, wasn't it? Let's go."

"You can finish the essay later, Quan. Go handle your business."

But what business is there for him to handle?

Quan doesn't say a word as he begins packing his school stuff—

"Leave it," the superintendent says, rotating on a heel. "I'll bring you back. Now hurry up." He disappears into the hallway.

After one final panicked glance in Doc's direction, Quan follows the superintendent out. They hang a right at the dead end—which surprises Quan: the visitation room is in the other direction.

"Uhh . . . sir? Not to question your sense of direction, but aren't we going the wrong way?"

The superintendent doesn't respond.

When they get to the end of *this* hallway, the super-intendent uses a key to buzz open a door Quan's never seen before. He follows the superintendent through, and then they hang one final left before the superintendent stops outside a room on the right. Door's open . . .

And Quan sees the *last* person he would've expected to make a pop-up visit:

His lawyer.

(If you can even call dude that. *Assigned file-handler* is probably more accurate.)

John Mark is his name. He's white. Late twenties. Took a public defender position fresh outta law school and been there for the two years since—Quan's case is his first time "legally flying solo" (his words).

Was Quan surprised the morning he came into one of the counsel rooms and found the young-looking dude sitting where his previous lawyer—who was actually good and seemed to really wanna *help* Quan—usually sat. John Mark stood and introduced himself. Let Quan know his previous counsel had moved out of state to take care of an elderly parent.

And it's not that John Mark is a *bad* lawyer. It just gets under Quan's skin a bit how . . . little the dude seems to question anything. It's like everything in the file is gospel, and there's nothing else to be said about it. Which, on the one hand, Quan can *kinda* get—he did confess (sorta) . . .

Still, though. Quan obviously knows there's way more to the story. Isn't it an attorney's job to poke around for more information?

Dude stands to greet Quan, grinning like all is right with the world.

Which is when the already tiny light that still burns inside Quan

goes a little dimmer.

"Vernell!" He shakes Quan's hand a little too vigorously.

"I told you to call me *Quan*, man."

"That's right, man, my bad." He runs a hand through his George Clooney haircut. *Jumpy as a jitterbug*, like Mrs. Pavlostathis used to say.

(He's been thinking of her more and more lately.)

"Anyway, have a seat, man—"

"Quan."

Dude blinks a few times. Goes pink in the cheeks.

Clears his throat.

"My apologies, Quan." Straightens his tie and pulls out a chair at the small table for Quan. "I have some news to share with you. Mind if we sit?"

Quan complies. His eyes roam the small room where **delinquents** like him (if you let the state tell it) convene with their attorneys. The cinder block walls are painted the bizarre cloudy yellow of snot and are totally bare.

And as lawyer dude takes his seat facing Quan and rests his elbows on his knees, fully in *professional* mode now, Quan's anxiety ratchets up even more.

"So," John Mark says all definitively, putting the tips of all

160

his fingers together like in the movies when the white dude in the suit means *business*.

Quan almost laughs.

Almost.

But then dude says something that rings in Quan's head like the

*********claaaaaaaaaaang*********

of his cell door

shutting him in

every night.

"I got a call from the prosecutor's office this morning," he continues.

And then he pauses. (For *dramatic effect*? Cuz it's working.)

He smiles again, then:

"They've offered you a plea bargain."

May 18

Dear Justyce,

Man. I don't even really know how to start this one. I got a
lotta . . . conflicting emotions happening right now.

On the one hand, I get my diploma tomorrow. Which I still
can't even really believe.

On the other, though . . . well, my "lawyer" popped up
yesterday. Came to tell me the state offered a plea deal on
my case.

Needless to say, ya boy was more than a little shocked. I've
been combing through Georgia legal code for weeks, tryna see
if my self-defense thing is feasible, and then boom. Shit's
crazy.

Long story short, they're offering to reduce the murder
charge to voluntary manslaughter and drop all the others.
("What others?" I can hear your Poindexter ass asking.
There were four: possession of a handgun by a minor,
possession of a firearm by a felon, pointing or aiming a
pistol at another, and discharge of a firearm on property of
another.)

I MIGHT be entitled to go back to juvenile court—though
either way, the sentence is up to twenty years—but my

162

attorney thinks they won't give me more than fifteen, and the possibility of parole won't be taken off the table.

I obviously didn't accept right then and there, but . . . I dunno, man. This complicates things a bit.

I've been thinking about it nonstop since dude put his crusty-ass hand on my shoulder as he stood to leave and said, "Just think about it." This is AFTER rambling on and on about how "solid" of a deal it is and how "blown away" he was when he heard it. "You could be outta here before your thirtieth birthday, man!"

He was so . . . chipper when he said that shit too. It really rubbed me the wrong way.

Anyway, I'd be lying if I said the deal isn't tempting. Hearing dude talk brought a lot of my anxiety—I got officially diagnosed with the "clinical" type, by the way—about going to trial right up to the surface. For some reasons I don't really get, I've been waiting on a trial date for over a year and a half, but hearing that offer made me realize how scared I am to actually be in a courtroom, at a defendant's table. In front of people who would be just fine with the state lockin' my ass up, grinding the key to dust, and sprinkling that shit over the ocean.

It's crazy to me that I'm even THINKING this, but maybe taking the deal wouldn't be a bad move. If things go well and I stay on my best behavior, I could be out in a decade or less. Which is WAY better than I was expecting, real talk.

I dunno.

Would love to hear what you think. Giving this letter to Doc to give to you since I know you not at school no more. Imma wait to hear back before I make my decision, so maybe try not to take TOO long to respond? (I'm still waiting for a response to the LAST letter I wrote your punk ass!)

—Q

Snapshot:

Two Boys, a Girl,
a Teacher, a Lawyer, and
a Case Management Intern
in a Basement

Standing beside the Friedman pool table with SJ grinning up at him from the Holy Land–made papasan chair, Jus almost feels like they're back prepping for a debate tournament.

Except this time, a young (almost) man's freedom is on the line.

He clears his throat.

"So, first off, thank you all for coming," he says to the room. Mrs. F—*Attorney Friedman* in her current capacity—is on the leather couch, fancy pen in hand and lawyerly leather notebook open on-lap; Doc and Liberty Ayers are on barstools; and Jared Christensen is perched on a chair he snagged from who knows where.

"As you all know, my homeboy Quan has been locked up since late September last year. For a crime that he did not, in fact, commit."

"Not to put a damper on your opening statement, Justyce, but how do you know that?" Doc asks.

"He told me. And I believe him."

Doc nods. "Go on. My apologies for interrupting."

Justyce smiles. "It's all good, Doc. I missed you, homie."

"Likewise, my man."

"So as I was saying, Quan didn't do the crime, but they're tryna give him *hella* time. The state offered to lessen the homicide charge—from murder to voluntary manslaughter in this case—and drop everything else if he pleads guilty. But that still carries a sentence of up to twenty years."

"Whew," from Doc.

"Normally I wouldn't be tellin' y'all my boy's business, but him having to serve even *one* year would be a tragic miscarriage of justice. The fact that he's been locked up for *this* long is a tragic miscarriage of justice."

"In-friggin-deed," from SJ.

"Now don't get me wrong," Justyce continues. "Despite my own unfortunate history with Officer Tomás Castillo, I do believe what happened to him was terrible, and that *true* justice should be served in his case. But this is not *true* justice. Imprisoning the wrong person is *not* true justice."

"PREACH, brutha!" Jared crows.

"So we gotta do something. Y'all with me?"

"Hell yeah we are!" from Jared again. Which makes SJ snort.

"Now, provided I can convince Quan to fire his current legal representative, Attorney Friedman here will take over his case. Which is why I called this conference. So we can all . . . confer. Anybody wanna jump in?"

Jared: So what exactly are we dealing with here?

SJ: Of course you're the first person to speak despite knowing the least. Of course—

168

Doc: Sarah-Jane—

Justyce: Actually, hold that thought. I'm being rude.

Justyce gestures to the deep-brown-skinned young lady with her locs wrapped in an elaborate knot on top of her head, sitting on the barstool beside Doc. She smiles in appreciation. (And Justyce could swear he sees SJ tense up out of the corner of his eye. Which is ridiculous. Yes, Liberty is absolutely gorgeous—even more so than he was expecting from Quan's letters. But it's not like Justyce *noticed* that . . .)

Justyce: Everyone, this is Liberty Ayers. She's one of the case managers on Quan's case—

Liberty: I'm an intern. But thank you. Doc I know, but it is lovely to meet the rest of you.

Jared: [*With stars in his eyes.*] Lovely to teet you moo, Liberty. I'm Jare—I mean meet tou yoo—crap.

SJ: [*Snorts.*] Looks like douchewangle's got a crush.

Jared: BRO!

Doc: [*Smiling as he shakes his head.*] I do not miss this foolishness in my classroom.

Justyce: [*Pretending he doesn't feel some type of way about what SJ said.*] Anyway, thank you for being here, Liberty.

Liberty: Wouldn't've missed it for the world.

Jared: You're an awesome intern, Liberty. Quan's lucky to have you in his corner.

SJ: Speaking of Quan, let's talk about him.

Justyce: [*Notices SJ's cheeks have gone a smidge pink, and she won't look at Liberty . . .*]

Justyce: [*Thinks,* Odd . . .]

SJ: What do we know?

Jared: He's a young African American man who's been radically short-changed by our criminal *IN*justice system.

SJ: [*Smacks forehead.*]

Doc: He's thoughtful. Dedicated. Fiercely loyal, even to a fault.

Liberty: You can say that again.

Attorney Friedman: What do you two mean by that?

Doc: Well, he's gone out of his way to protect whoever did shoot Tomás Castillo. Even beyond implicating himself and staying mum about the shooter's identity, he refused the legal counsel offered by the leader of the . . . *organization* he was a part of because he didn't want any connections that could link back to his associates.

Justyce: I didn't know that.

Doc: Don't think he wanted you to.

Liberty: I know this mentality well. I was gang-affiliated when I was younger.

Jared: [*Perking up like Liberty just confessed to being Santa Claus.*] You were?

Liberty: I was. And even beyond the whole snitches get stitches and/or ditches concept that's almost a joke to *most* people who say it—

(Justyce could swear Liberty glances at oblivious Jared when she says that.)

Liberty:—when you grow up feeling like no one's on your side, and you suddenly find people who are, it literally changes your brain. That loyalty Quan feels isn't merely a choice. It's a psychological imperative.

170

Attorney Friedman: [*Jotting notes.*] So I'll steer clear of anything that would make him think I want him to throw a friend under the bus. What else?

Justyce: The gun they found with Quan's prints on it wasn't the one that fired the deadly shots, so the ballistics won't match.

Jared: Isn't that something they would've checked before making an arrest?

Attorney Friedman: Not necessarily. If a firearm was found on the scene, I'm sure the moment they matched the prints to a name, a warrant was issued and that was that. Ballistics were likely run in forensics, but there's a chance the report was hidden in the midst of a large discovery dump, especially if the bullets pulled from the body didn't match the caliber of the weapon found on the scene.

Justyce: Quan also mentioned wanting to try for a self-defense plea. Says Castillo first had his gun pointed at Martel, then swung it around to where Quan was standing with his boys. Which is when someone shot him.

Attorney Friedman: Martel?

Justyce: One of the "friends" you definitely shouldn't mention.

Attorney Friedman: Got it. So Castillo pointed his weapon at multiple people that night. Sounds like voluntary manslaughter should've been the charge in the first place. [*She scribbles more notes.*] Was there provocation? Any reason for Castillo to pull the firearm?

Justyce: Quan says no. And there are a whole lot of witnesses who would say the same thing.

Attorney Friedman: The other guys who were there. That he doesn't want to implicate.

Justyce: Yeah.

Attorney Friedman: How many of the potential witnesses have extensive juvenile criminal records like Quan?

Justyce: Probably all of them.

Attorney Friedman: [*Nodding.*] As much as I hate it, if this goes to trial, and most of my witnesses are African American males between sixteen and twenty—just like the defendant who's accused of murdering a cop—implicit bias is likely to come into play.

Liberty: You can say that again. Happens all the time in the social work sector. Say a mom is trying to get her kids back. She's gotten cleaned up and has a steady job and is really working hard. If she's poor and African American and all the people vouching for her are poor and African American too . . . Well, I've seen more than a few cases where those kids wind up in long-term foster care.

Jared: But would you really need more than one or two witnesses? It's not like the state has any to dispute the testimony.

SJ: Huh?

Jared: The only person who could've been a key witness is dead, right?

Everyone: [*Silence.*]

Jared: Wasn't Garrett Tison killed in prison? Unless somebody else who was there that night is willing to testify against Quan, there's really no one who could dispute his story.

Everyone: [*More silence.*]

Attorney Friedman: Huh. Must admit: I didn't think of that.

SJ: That might be the most intelligent thing you've ever said, Jared.

Doc: Is there a chance a neighbor saw something and could come forward?

Attorney Friedman: I'll double-check, but I'd think they would've presented themselves by now. I'm sure everyone on the street was questioned.

Justyce: So . . . it's settled then. The prosecution doesn't really have anything. You think that's why they offered the plea deal?

SJ: Jus, babe, you're forgetting something.

Doc: SJ's right. The no-witness thing is a step, but even with that and a ballistics fail, this case isn't as cut-and-dried as you want it to be, Jus.

Justyce: Why isn't it?

SJ: Because Quan confessed.

Justyce: But he was lying!

SJ: Doesn't matter.

Attorney Friedman: Unfortunately, she's right, Justyce. Especially in this case. State's got no reason not to believe him.

Justyce: So that's it? We let him take the plea and serve time for something he didn't do?

Doc: Take a breath, Jus. That's not what Attorney Friedman said.

Attorney Friedman: A confession isn't a plea, but since it's still admissible in court—

Justyce: [*Furrowing his brows.*] Unless it isn't.

SJ: Huh?

Justyce: Meeting adjourned. There's something I gotta do. [*Pushes off the edge of the pool table and heads for the stairs.*]

SJ: Oh boy.

Jared: ATTAGUY, J-MAN!

Liberty: [*Whispering to Doc.*] Is Jared always like this?

Doc: Pretty much.

Liberty: Yeesh.

9

Dawg

Quan's in his cell, flipping through one of the poetry collections Doc dropped off, when he hears his name barked out like he stole something.

"BANKS!"

Shocks him so bad, he drops the book *and* falls off the bed.

Also takes too long to respond, apparently. He can hear the heavy footsteps approaching just before his least-favorite guard's glistening bald head pokes through the open doorway.

More barking.

"You don't hear me calling you, fool?"

"I heard you, I heard you," Quan says, rubbing his knee. (These concrete floors are *rough*.) "Just startled me is all."

"Well, bring your raggedy ass on." (Bark, bark, bark.) **"You got a visitor."**

"A visitor?"

(Awww, damn. Who could it be thi—)

"That's what I said, ain't it? You punk-asses act like you can't understa—"

But Quan doesn't hear any more.

What if it's his lawyer again? Back to demand a decision about the plea offer.

Which Quan hasn't made yet. He's waiting to hear back from Justyce, and it's been less than forty-eight hours since Quan gave the letter to Doc to pass on. He's gotta give his boy at least a *little* more time.

They reach the turnoff to head down the hallway where lawyer meetings happen—and keep going.

Now Quan's really confused.

Clearly ain't Doc. Baldy knows who *he* is and would've taken Quan to the classroom wing. So who—?

The sound of the visitation room door buzzing open snaps Quan back into his body. Baldy steps aside to let him enter . . .

And now Quan thinks his head might explode. And his chest.

His . . . everything.

"Dawg!" Justyce says, standing up and spreading his arms.

Takes everything in Quan not to

RUN

over to the table.

(He successfully resists.)

"Bruh, what're you *doing* here?" Quan asks once he

176

reaches Justyce. They slap hands, hook fingers, and pull into one of the best dap-hugs Quan's ever experienced.

"Hey, BREAK IT UP!"

But nothing that hatin'-ass mahogany-bowling-ball-head has to say could bring Quan down now.

"I had to come see you, man." The boys take their seats, and Justyce looks left and then right. (Quan snorts and shakes his head. Justyce has no concept of *smooth*.) "I got your letters."

"I would hope so, fool!" Quan says, trying to keep things light.

But Justyce ain't lookin' real playful. He peeks around again and leans forward. "Dawg, you gotta fire your lawyer."

"Huh?"

"Don't make a scene, man." Though Justyce is really the one making a scene. Whispering and tryna be all clandestine and shit.

Quan takes a realignment breath.

Why is this visit becoming so stressful?

"Justyce, you know you my boy, but you can't pop up here making declarations like that without some kinda lead-in."

Justyce nods. "Okay, man. You right. I'm sorry."

"It's cool."

A fitful, sparky tension blooms between them. Like a thundercloud trapped in a jar. One good lightning strike, and the whole thing'll shatter.

"Lemme start over," Justyce says.

"Yeah. *Expound* if you will, please."

Both boys laugh, and the walls seem to exhale.

"So, I got your letters," Justyce says.

Quan nods. "Got that part."

"I was shocked by the first one. Where you told me . . . the thing. About the thing. But once it settled in, I wasn't entirely surprised."

"Okay."

"I obviously respect you not wanting to uhh . . . say more." The boys lock eyes, and understanding passes between them. "But having *read* that first letter, what you mention in the most recent one was troubling."

Quan clenches his jaw. Of course Justyce doesn't get his predicament. Why would he? Justyce McAllister has always had options.

Choices—

"Some friends and I wanna help," Justyce continues. "We got a new lawyer for you. A good one. She's actually my girl's mom, and she's worked on a lotta cases like yours."

"Cases 'like mine'?"

Justyce nods, either oblivious to Quan's irritation or ignoring it. "Young black dude gets caught up in some wrong place/wrong time shenanigans and winds up behind bars because of it."

Quan shakes his head.

Shenanigans.

Justyce *would* use that word. What's the other one Doc taught him? **Understatement**? Like "*Somebody findin' out* _____ *actually pulled the trigger would be bad.*"

Shenanigans.

Bad.

Understatements.

"I can't do it, man. I can't have nobody goin' after my crew because of me—"

"No one else would be implicated, man. You have my word on that. Based solely on what you've told me so far, there should be enough evidence to get you acquitted."

Quan bites the inside of his cheek. The choice between an acquittal and a decade in prison is obviously a no-brainer . . . but there's still a chance he'll be convicted. Especially with his prior record. Walking away from the deal means walking away from the lesser charge. And being convicted of **murder**? Especially one he really didn't commit?

"I just—" (There Justyce goes, peeping over his shoulders all suspiciously again.)

"You gotta stop doing that, man," Quan says. "Glancing around like you tryna hide something. That'll get *both* of us in trouble up in here."

"Oh."

"Go ahead and say what you gotta say. *Without* looking like a stage four creep, please."

Justyce laughs a little. "You right, man. My bad. I'm just nervous is all."

Which makes *Quan* nervous.

And Quan hates being nervous. "About?"

"Well, I need you to tell me *more* about . . . something."

"So spit it out, fool!"

(Now Quan's tempted to peep over his *own*
shoulder.)

Justyce sighs. "I need you to tell me about your confession, man."

Oh.

"What about it?" Quan can feel what Tay calls his *barriers* beginning to rise.

"Like . . . how it happened. *When* it happened. Did they show up on the scene and you stepped forward?"

Quan shakes his head, tense about reliving the whole thing. His palms have gone slicker than the game he's seen Trey spit at the girls up the block. "Nah. They didn't come and arrest me until a few days after . . . everything happened."

"You mentioned an interrogation in one of your letters . . . Did you confess before they took you?"

"Nope." Quan tries to relax his jaw. "They had a warrant."

"So what the hell happened, man?"

There's a sour taste in Quan's mouth now, and what he really wants to do is wave Brown Bowling Ball over to strike on through this visit and escort him back to his gutter-esque cellblock. Which oddly seems safer than this open room with Justyce asking him these *questions*. But looking at his boy—in the flesh—and seeing how much dude *cares* . . . well, that's not something Quan was distinctly prepared for.

So he takes yet another deep breath and drops himself back into the night he more or less ruined his own life.

First time they questioned me, I ain't really say nothin'. I do know my rights—that was one thing Martel was real big on—so once they had me in the room at the precinct and started asking questions, I told them I was choosing to remain silent, and left it at that.

They left me in the room by myself at that point, and I don't know how long I sat in that hard-ass chair with my hands cuffed behind me, but I started to fall asleep. It was like ten-something at night when they initially picked me up, so I knew it was getting late, and I was tired. I also hadn't eaten in a while. Appetite was real spotty during them days after The Occurrence. That's what Tay's been having me call it.

Anyway, eventually somebody else came in and they took me to a cell. I really wanted to just go to sleep—it was a couple other dudes in there knocked out—so I sat down and leaned my head against the bars. But it seemed like every time I was almost asleep, there would be a noise or a laugh or something that would wake my ass right up.

A bunch more time passed, and a new officer came and got me. Female this time.

I said the same shit I said the first time.

They left me alone again. Then back to the holding cell I went.

More of the same: almost falling asleep, but not being able to. Getting more and more hungry. That second time in the holding cell is when I could feel myself starting to crack a little bit. I was tired. Cold. Needed to pee. Scared of what was gonna happen.

Third time they pulled me into the room started out like the other two. I told them I ain't have nothing to say, but that time, they wouldn't leave me alone. It was the same dude from the first time. I guess enough time had passed for him to be on the clock again. He kept pushin'. Come on, kid. We know you did it. Might as well just say so . . . shit like that.

When he said You know if we get one of your little buddies in here, we can get 'em talkin'. You should just save 'em the trouble, that's when I broke. Just said

Fine, man. I did it. You happy now?

When Quan looks up—swiping at his eyes (he's never told anybody the story of what happened that night and this is exactly why)—Justyce has a thinky face on: eyebrows all scrunched up, jaw tight, gaze on Quan but not *on* Quan. "And you said you told them the same thing each time they questioned you?"

"Yeah. Basically."

182

"Even the third time, you said *I'm choosing to remain silent?*"

That query makes Quan itchy for some reason. "I mean, I don't remember if I said exactly that, but it was clear I ain't wanna talk."

"Okay," Justyce says with a finality that lets Quan know he can shut the door on that night again.

(Though he's definitely gonna have to talk to Tay about it now. After opening *that* vault, he knows he's gonna have nightmares.)

"Cut that sorry excuse you have for a lawyer loose, and let's get things headed in a more favorable direction," Justyce says.

Quan sighs and rubs his eyes. He wishes he could just . . . sleep. Indefinitely. All this shit is too much. "I don't know, man. That's a tall order. I haven't even met this *replacement* you tryna give me."

"You gotta trust me, Quan," Justyce presses. "She's a really great attorney. And you wouldn't lose your plea offer."

Now Quan's ears perk up. "I wouldn't?"

"Nope. She'd make sure of it. Might even be able to get you a better one if it comes to that. Based on everything you've told me, it sounds like you were overcharged."

This makes Quan smile. "Oh, so *you* a lawyer now, smarty pants? One year up in bougie-and-educated land, and you ready to take on my case?"

Justyce smiles back. "I'm working on it."

"TIME'S UP!" (Bark bark.)

"Guess that's my cue." Justyce stands.

And

Quan's

chest

tightens.

"Yeah. Guess it is," he says. (But Justyce *just* got here, didn't he? Damn.)

"You're gonna do it, right?"

"BANKS! I know your punk ass heard me!"

Quan glances over his shoulder at angry Baldy.

Is it really possible he could get outta here?

He stands.

And ponders.

And ponders a little more.

"You sure about all this, man?" he finally says, reaching out to dap Justyce up.

"HEY! None of that gang shit in here! You 'bout to lose your visitation privile—"

"Would I be here if I weren't?"

Quan looks at Justyce.

Justyce looks at Quan.

And understanding passes between them.

184

June 1

Dear Justyce,

So I did it, as I'm sure you know. Cut John Mark like a loose thread (which honestly is kind of what he was) and had my case turned over to your girl's mom.

Adrienne.

(Do you call her that, by the way? She insisted I should, but shit's weird, and I feel like my mama would smack the taste out my mouth if she heard me refer to a grown woman—a professional grown woman at that—by her first name.)

ANYWAY.

I met her today. She came in and we talked for a while and she asked me a bunch of questions the other dude never asked. And I'm pretty sure she actually believes everything I told her. Which was even a little bit uncomfortable despite the fact that I was telling the truth.

I just didn't realize what a difference it would make to be in conversation with someone who genuinely wants to keep me OUT of prison altogether. Shit made me realize that in all my years dealing with the system, I ain't never had an attorney who wanted to see me totally free. It kinda got me thinking about some of the dudes I've met over the years who

185

wound up getting put away for a long time. Not like we ever sat around talking about our problems in a Kumbaya circle or anything, but I know a lot of us were similar: home lives that were messed up (or "high trauma" if you let Liberty tell it. Bruh, the pantsuit she had on when she came by the other day . . . whew!); people all around expecting us to blow it at some point; no adult role models . . .

And like, none of that is an excuse, but now that I find myself with all these people in my life who believe I've got some good in me and want to see me live it out . . . well, I'm scared, man. I don't even know who I AM right now, writing you all this feely shit, but it's true.

Ms. Adrienne (ain't no way I can call that lady JUST by her first name!) made a statement at the end of our meeting that still has me shook: "We're on your side, Quan. Our goal is to get you out of here and reintegrated into society as a vital contributor to the betterment of the world."

But what if I can't "reintegrate," Justyce? What even do I have TO "contribute"? It's not like I haven't tried to be and do good. Like yeah, when I was like fourteen, fifteen, I stopped caring cuz it didn't really seem like anybody cared about ME. But it took some years for me to get to that point, you know? Years of caring. And trying. And failing. And not knowing what to do about it or how to fix it. Cuz I was trying, Justyce. I was trying so damn hard.

Like I'm looking back now, and SO MANY OF US who wind up in here really did WANT to do shit the right way and be

186

"successful." But there's so many other things dudes like us be contending with. Again, not saying that's an excuse, but I also can't sit here and pretend like the shit doesn't matter.

It's this new dude on my cellblock, Berto. Latino dude. He's been here for about a month now. I got him talking the other day—bruh, dude didn't talk to NOBODY his first few weeks up in here—and he's 16 and in for a murder charge as well. But he was telling me how growing up, he was this real good kid, until some stuff happened in his family.

So he went looking for a _new_ family. Like a lot of us do. Same story with another dude we call Stacks. He's constantly talking about "this guy" he knows (aka himself) and how "he was workin' to become a musician," but "he was young and ain't have no guidance"; how "he just wanted a family so he went and found one," but then "he got in trouble doing family shit."

And that's what it comes down to. We find the families we were desperate for and learn different ways of going about things. Ways that sometimes land us in places/positions we don't really wanna be in.

What if I can't shake that? What if I get outta here and then wind up in the wrong place at the wrong time again? What if I disappoint everybody going to bat for me right now? What do I even have to offer the world, Justyce? Like if I get out for REAL for real, what am I actually gonna DO?

And I hate that I'm even thinking about this shit. That I'm afraid I won't be able to stay outta trouble.

That I'm even considering what life will be like back on the outside.

Because what if this doesn't work and "hope" fails me again and I get locked up . . . for life?

I don't know if I'll be able to handle that, man.

Sincerely,

Quan

Snapshot:

A Prelaw Yale Undergrad,
a Defense Lawyer,
and a District Attorney
in a Law Office

Despite being here to *oppose* him in a sense, Justyce would be lying if he said he wasn't in awe of Attorney Marcus Anthony Baldwin Sr. The DA is tall and fit and stately. Warm, but clearly about his business. Jovial, but take-no-shit. A man whose presence commands full attention and utmost respect.

And he's black.

Justyce is sure he didn't imagine the little flicker of pride on the man's face when Attorney Friedman introduced Justyce as one of her "undergraduate interns who just completed his first prelaw year at Yale."

And now? Justyce has the man's full attention.

"So you've been in communication with the defendant, young man?" the DA asks.

"Yes, sir. I have. We've known each other since childhood but began corresponding through letters in January."

"Do you intend to enter any of these letters into evidence, Adrienne?"

"I do not."

The DA's head tilts just the slightest bit. "You don't?"

"Genuinely don't think it'll be necessary," Attorney Friedman says.

Attorney Baldwin: "Interesting."

"We're actually here about some things he expressed to me in person," Justyce continues.

"In person?"

"Yes, sir. I paid him a visit at the detention center about a week ago, and he shared some information that I believe warrants further investigation."

Now Attorney Baldwin leans back in his fancy leather desk chair. Clasps his hands over his midsection. "I'm listening."

"Well, the first thing he said is that the firearm found at the scene and used to identify him wasn't the one that fired the fatal shot."

Baldwin's eyebrows leap up to attention.

"Do you know if ballistics were run, Marcus?" Attorney Friedman says. "I didn't see any reports in the files that were turned over to me. There's a confession on record, yes, but considering the severity of the charges here, I feel it vital to carry out a *full* investigation with due diligence."

Baldwin puts his hands up. "I hear you. It'll probably take a few weeks, but I'll make sure the proper tests are ordered. However, as you just mentioned, with an admission of guilt on file—"

"That's the other thing," Justyce says, cutting Attorney Baldwin off.

And immediately regretting it. "Oh, man. My apologies, sir. I didn't mean to—"

"Go on, Mr. . . . McAllister, is it?"

"Yes, sir. Uhhh . . ." Now Jus has to get back on his game.

He clears his throat. "As I was saying, when I last spoke with Vernell, we had a brief discussion about the particulars of his confession, and . . . well, I think the *circumstances* surrounding said confession could use a closer look."

"And what exactly would we be looking for, Mr. McAllister?"

Without thinking, Justyce looks at Attorney Friedman.

"You're in my office with my full consideration, Mr. McAllister. You don't need Attorney Friedman's permission to speak. Go on, please."

Justyce takes a deep breath. "Based on what Qua—I mean *Vernell* told me, sir, I think his Miranda rights may have been violated."

Now Justyce *really* has the DA's "full consideration." Feels like he's on a slide that's just been clipped into place beneath the lens of a microscope. "Is that right?" the man says, picking up a pair of glasses from the desk and sliding them onto his face before opening a drawer to pull out a legal pad. (Justyce almost laughs at this.)

"Yes, sir."

Attorney Baldwin scribbles some stuff. "Well, you have my word that we will thoroughly investigate the matters you've brought to my attention."

"Thank you, sir."

Baldwin tosses his pen on the desk, removes his glasses, and looks Jus in the eye. Jus wants to look away posthaste but forces himself not to.

"You picked a good one, Adrienne," Baldwin says.

"Don't I know it," from Attorney Friedman.

"You've got a bright future ahead of you, Mr. McAllister," Attorney Baldwin continues. "Vernell's lucky to have you as a friend. It's unfortunate, but in the majority of cases like this one, the young men involved don't have any true advocates. I commend you for coming forward."

"Just don't want to see another African American boy wind up in prison, especially for a crime he didn't commit," Jus replies, feeling a burst of boldness shoot up inside him, strong and steady. "As a person committed to the dispensation of *true* justice, I hope you feel the same way, sir."

Attorney Baldwin draws back the teeniest bit and *blinkblinkblinks*. And out of the corner of his eye, Justyce sees Mrs. F "cough" into her fist.

"Ahh . . ." Attorney Baldwin clears his throat. "Yes. I most certainly do, young man."

"Thrilled to hear it."

There's a beat of silence that feels to Justyce like an invisible balloon full of confetti is about to burst overhead and shower the room in his sense of triumph. Then:

"Is there anything else I can do for the two of you?" from Attorney Baldwin.

"I think that covers everything, sir," Jus replies.

And Mrs. F just grins.

10

Dasia

Despite the "meeting" *Quan* was pulled into—with Liberty *and* Tay—in preparation for this week's visitor, each step up the corridor makes him feel that much closer to the chopping block for a beheading.

> (Maybe shouldn't've read *Alice's Adventures in Wonderland* last night.)

It's gotta be bad.

Like *has* to be.

It's not just the fact that she hasn't visited *once* in the twenty-one months he's been in here.

She also never answers when he calls—which he made a point of doing at least once every couple weeks for the entire first *year* he was locked up.

She hasn't sent any letters. Or care packages.

Which means whatever she's coming to tell Quan is so bad,

> she feels the need to say it

to

his

face.

And he ain't ready.

But it doesn't matter. Because the superintendent has stopped and the door is opening and her chin is lifting. Eyes widen, mouth opens—

"Ain't got all day, Banks . . . ,"

the superintendent says.

Because Quan's still standing in the

doorway.

Looking at his mama. His mama whose chin seems to be quivering in time with the drumroll sound of his own heart-beat in his ears. He can't even force down one of his special recentering breaths the way Tay told him to when she and Liberty were "preparing" him.

The meeting/session/whatever the hell you wanna call it was strange for Quan. It was his first time in who-knows-how-long sharing a space with two women at once, and see-ing the rapport between them, the way they fed off each other in pursuit of *"the optimal circumstances"* for his *"mental and emotional well-being"* shook him down to his molecules.

"So," Liberty said as she sat down across from him in one of the cushy chairs that takes up the center of the office space where Quan has his regular counseling sessions with Tay.

(Libz was wearing this long yellow dress and had

her hair tied up in this dope wrap-thing that

reminded Quan of the kente-print shirts Martel sometimes wore. Made Quan feel he was being addressed by the sun. Actually makes him feel a little better in *this* moment to think about her.)

"First I want to apologize for inserting myself into your weekly session," Liberty began.

(*Like I mind*, Quan thought.)

"But Tay and I agreed that this was important enough to break with routine," she continued.

Tay nodded.

Quan smiled. Basking in the sunlight.

And then:

"Your mom called the facility to ask about visitation hours," Liberty said.

Quan went hot all over.

"Ms. Bernice, who works at the front desk and received the call, immediately reached out to me after checking the visitation log and seeing that this would be your mom's first time coming."

"And then Libby immediately reached out to *me*," Tay said.

Over the next hour, they "discussed." Was Quan okay taking the visit? (He was allowed to refuse.) Did he feel ready to see his mother? Was there anything he wanted to talk about or work through prior? Did he have any questions?

And he did:

Why now?

What does she want?

Does this mean she still cares?

Then why don't she answer my calls?

But he didn't ask any of them. Because the overriding one is still clanging around in his brain like an eight-alarm fire alert as he crosses the visitation space:

What happened?

She doesn't get up when he reaches the table, and it occurs to Quan how good it is that the thing is cemented to the ground. Because watching her sit there and cry like she's suddenly *moved* by the sight of him makes Quan want to flip the whole shit over.

He sits without a word.

Even with her brown skin, Quan can see the dark circles beneath her eyes. She's lost weight too. More gray in her hair.

She wipes her face and smiles. Sort of.

And then they just sit. For who knows how long.

Staring.

At each other.

Quan's certainly not gonna be the one to break the silence so—

"Gabe misses you," his mama says, and she might as well have dropped a bucket of ice water on his head.

He'd get up and walk away if not for the fact that it's his *mama*.

And beneath all his fury,

he still wants her to love him.

198

"What you here for, Ma?" he says, and her gaze plummets to the table. *Through* the table, even.

"I'm not tryna be rude," Quan goes on, "but in all honesty, you popping up out the blue like this has me a little shaken. So if we could avoid dragging this whole thing out—"

Quan stops, not wanting to go any further. He's sure that stung—it pricked *his* throat on the way up. He knows if he keeps talking, all the mama-related rage he hasn't gotten to in his sessions with Tay will shoot off his tongue in sharp-edged words.

Mama sighs. "Your sister is sick, LaQuan."

"Huh?"

> (Though of course he heard exactly what she
> said.)
>> (He wasn't expecting her to just *give in* to
>> his . . . aggression.)

"Dasia was diagnosed with leukemia a few weeks ago."

Now Quan has

NO IDEA

what to say.

"It's pretty aggressive, and she starts chemo next week . . ."

Quan opens his mouth to speak this time, but it's no use: the rest comes pouring out of Mama like hot coffee gulped down too fast, scalding her mouth on the way out, searing a path into the table and burning Quan's hands and arms as it overflows the edge into his lap.

199

FirstDoctorWeWentToSaidTheChemoWasPointless."There's
NoWayWeCouldGetItAll.SheMaybeHasTwo/ThreeMonthsTo
Live."ButYouKnowYourSister,StubbornSinceTheDaySheWas
Born—Ain'tEvenReallyWannaComeOutINTOthisCrazyWorld—
AnywaySheRefusedToHearThat "Bull"AndDemandedWeSeek
OutASecondOpinion.PrognosisWasBetter—IThinkItProbably
HelpedThatTheSecondDoctorWasABlackWomanWhoActually
GaveADamnWhetherOrNotMyBabyGirlLivesOrDies.ButThe
PointIsEvenWithALessShittyDoctor,CancerIsStillCancerAin'tIt?
It'sExpensiveAndTime-ConsumingAndWeWereUninsuredAt
FirstAndThoughWeGotTheInsuranceNowAndIt'sRetroactive,I
RecentlyLostMyJob,LikeLastWeek.JustSoHappenedThatThe
NextDay,YourFriendCameByToCheckOnUsCuzHeSai—

"*My* 'friend'? What friend is that?"

    Montrey, she says.

      (And now there's a new little stab of rage—
        and maybe even fear—in Quan's gut.)

        (Ain't like he heard any more from his "friends"
         than he did from Mama . . .)

        (But does this mean *they* haven't forgotten
         about him either?)

LikeIWasSaying,MontreyCameByCuzHeSaidHeSawGabeIn
ThePark"LookinAllSad,"SoHeWantedToMakeSureEverything
WasOkayAnd—

    IDunnoWhatHappened . . .

She's wholly in her own world now. REliving as she REcalls. Which makes the whole thing, and the fact that she's sitting here in front of him sharing it, seem a little less RIdiculous.

EverythingJust . . . CameOutIGuess,IWasSoStressedOutAnd Hadn'tBeenSleeping.NextThingIKnow,I'mCryin'AndMontreyIs Huggin'MeAndHe'sSayingSomethingAboutHow"YouKnow AnyFamOfQuanIsFamOfOurs"And"WeGonMakeSureY'all TakenCareOfMs.Trish,"ThenHeLeftAndAFewHoursLater HeAndAFewOfYourOtherFriendsShowedUpWithGroceries AndMadeMeGetOffMyFeetAndAGirlHeIntroducedAs "MyLadyHere"CameInAndCookedDinnerAndCleanedUpAnd TheyLEFTAnEnvelopeWithEnoughMoneyToGetUsThrough TheMonthAndIDon'tKnowWhereTheMoneyComesFromAnd Ain'tSureIReallyWantToBut—

She shakes her head, realizing where she is, and seems to slip back into her body. Quan's been staring at her the whole time, and they finally look at each other.

He *definitely* ain't got nothing to say now.

"Anyway," Mama says, breaking the eye contact. "Sorry for shakin' you up by coming here. I just—"

(Please let her say she wanted to see me . . .

Quan thinks.)

"Well, I just thought you should know." She sniffs. Turns away from him now. And Quan knows right then he won't feel his mama's gaze on him again. "About your sister."

"She know you were coming to tell me?" he says, though he already knows the answer.

He watches her chest rise and fall with force. "She didn't really want you to know."

"I figured. Well, thanks for telling me anyway. Not much I can do, obviously—" though I wish there was more, he doesn't say.

She nods. Just once.

"Gabe really does miss you, though."

Quan smiles in spite of himself. "Tell li'l man I miss him too. Imma see him soon—" It's past his lips and dangling in the air out of reach before he can snatch it back.

HOPE.

Now Mama's eyes *do* latch on to him again. Skeptically. And maybe even a little . . . protectively.

But not of him.

"Yeah, okay, LaQuan," she says, clearly *done* with the conversation. She rises from the table. "You take care of yourself in here."

Done.

It almost chokes him on the way out—especially after hearing her give up on him again—but Quan manages a "Yes, ma'am."

His mama motions to let a guard know she's

done.

"Just wanted you to know stuff ain't been easy, but everything's all right."

As she walks away, though? Without a single glance behind her?

Quan wants to cry out:

How can anything be "all right" when me being HERE is all wrong?

June 14

Dear Justyce,

I'm . . . not in a great place right now. Found out some shit about my sister and . . . man, I don't even know.

So my moms came through—with bad news obviously, cuz why the hell else would she pay a visit to her wrongfully incarcerated firstborn. And looking PAST the fact that it dredged up all this unresolved "mommy-issue" shit I know Tay is gonna be riding my ass about for the next who-knows-how-long, the stuff Mama TOLD me threw me into such a damn tailspin, I had a full-blown panic attack in the hallway on the way back to my cell. I think the superintendent almost shit his pants.

"Damn, homie. What exactly did she tell you?" I can hear your goofy ass saying (which actually makes me feel a little lighter, won't lie). The long and short of it is that my crew has been helping her out.

I was real surprised at first. Truth be told, I thought all them fools had moved on. Washed their hands of your boy and went on about their lives. Guess it's safe to say Tay's prolly right about me having some sorta abandonment complex.

(Pause: not sure how I feel about the fact that my counselor pretty much lives inside my head now.)

Anyway, like I was saying, I guess deep down I've been convinced that everybody I really gave a damn about—in what feels like a whole other life—has forgotten about me. Can't none of them visit me obviously, but my moms never did either. And the only person who's ever written to me in here is you.

And fine: I can't imagine none of my dudes sitting down to handwrite no letter. Even knowing all that, though, after a while, the silence makes a dude start to think certain things.

Hearing that they not only <u>haven't</u> blotted my existence from their memories, but are helping take care of my family when I can't? That shit has me ALL messed up, man.

Not sure if you read poetry (if you don't, you should. Doc got me hooked.), but there's this one stanza from a poem by this dude named Jason Reynolds that keeps coming back to me:

> *jason jason grind and grit*
> *don't forget you're not alone*
> *for everywhere is where you fit*
> *and everyone feels just the same*

It's actually a poem about going too hard and being tired and needing a rest, but seeing my mama reminded me of what it felt like to be held down by dudes who <u>got</u> me. Knew where I came from, understood what I been through, and held me down even when my own mama had given up on me. The fact that they're now holding HER down, just because she's connected to me . . . That's got me feeling some type of way, man.

All I can think about now is if (when?) I DO get outta here, don't I gotta go back?

Wouldn't a real man ensure that his debts are paid? That those who stood in for him are shown appreciation not only through his words, but through his deeds?

Guess I just feel like I owe them the same kind of loyalty they showing me by making sure my moms and brother are taken care of while my sister goes through what she gotta go through.

Hell, by the time I leave this place, Imma owe them more than just loyalty.

What am I supposed to do about that? What am I supposed to do at all? Even if I am granted a favorable verdict in the case, I still got felonies on my record. I been in and outta jail since I was thirteen, man. Who's gonna give me a job? And before you throw some "Go to college!" shit at me, who's gonna pay for it?

ALL of that aside, even if I managed to go to college AND get a job, I can't just walk away from my crew. Number one, it don't work like that. Even if I didn't owe them a thing, I couldn't just bounce. I've seen and know too much, man.

This is a real-ass Catch-22. I read that shit a couple weeks ago. (HELLA trippy book.) The only way to stay OUT of what I really have no choice but to go back to is to stay IN here. But the longer I'm IN here, the more debt I'll rack up for when I do get OUT.

Kind of a no-win, ain't it?

Story of my damn life.

—Q

Snapshot:

A Black Boy
(and a White Boy)
Visits a Black Man
(and a White Boy)

Jared insisted on coming. Said it would be "both enlighten-
ing and educational," and that he needed "greater familiarity
with the population" he'd "eventually be serving."

But as he and Justyce walk up the driveway of their destination, and Jus sees the smile that splits the face of his old
pal Montrey Filly—who has grown a beard since the last
time Jus saw him . . . which was also the last time Jus was
here—a memory of Jared's Halloween experiment-gone-
wrong senior year *POPS* into Justyce's head with the force
and speed of a gunshot.

This was a *terrible* idea.

"Smarty Pants!" Trey calls out, spreading his arms. "I see
you brought a friend?"

Jus gulps down the panic making his legs want to move
backward and shoves ahead even though it feels like wading
through wet concrete.

"'Sup, Trey?" Justyce says as they reach the foot of the
porch steps. "This is Jared. He, uhh, wanted to meet y'all."

Just then, Brad comes out of the house, grinning. He's
also got some hair on his face now. And fuzzy blond locs that
really are *dreadful*.

Which makes Justyce think of something else: last he
heard, both of these guys had been arrested for arson. He

wonders when they got out. (Perhaps that "organization" lawyer Doc said Quan rejected is good at what he does.)

He also wonders if one of them is Tomás Castillo's true killer.

"Justyce here was just introducing me to his pal," Trey says to Brad.

And Jared's dumb ass sticks out a hand to shake. "Jared," he says. "Nice grill, man," and he gestures to his own teeth.

"I know what a grill is and where it goes, fool," Brad replies.

"Yo, I know you from somewhere?" Trey says to Jared. "You look hella familiar . . ."

"Smart guy, ain't this one of them clowns you showed up at that party with Halloween before last?" from Brad.

"Oh yeaaaaah, that's right." Trey's rubbing his beard with his eyes narrowed all menacingly now.

Again: terrible idea.

"You can go on in, Justyce," Trey continues. So Jus and Jared ascend the three stairs. But then: "White boy stays out here with us, though."

All of Justyce's vital organs drop down into his sneakers, but to his surprise, when he peeks over his shoulder at Jared, dude is beaming like Trey just offered him his very own planet full of "hot tamales," as Jared's prone to call beautiful women.

(Real work-in-progress, that guy.)

Despite Jared's apparent comfort—Justyce swears he

212

hears him say "So about the Halloween thing . . ." as he's headed up Martel's ancient Kemet–enshrined hallway—Jus really has to focus to keep his heart rate from climbing to the speed of instant death. He did his research on gang exit strategies and discovered a number of . . . troubling things. (*Jumped in/stabbed out* came up a few more times than he's expressly comfortable with.)

Knowing what he's here to ask Martel is—

Well, it's likely he's lost his damn mind, so he's trying real hard not to think about it.

"Well, well, well," Martel says as Justyce steps into the living room. He's in his personal papasan just as Justyce expected him to be, but clad in all black today. He's grown out his hair a bit, and it's cut into a Mohawk-type thing Jus has to admit is pretty dope. Also mustachioed and bearded, but cut real close to his skin. "Good to have you back, young brutha."

Justyce's eyes drop to Martel's ankle.

"I'm a free man now," Martel says, startling Jus so bad, he flinches.

Which of course is just *hilarious* to the older dude. "I see you haven't changed much," he says. "College treatin' you good?"

"It's all right," Jus says with a shrug.

"Guessin' that's not what you here to talk about, though . . ."

Justyce's gaze gets pulled to the floor as if by a magnet.

"I'll admit, I was surprised when you called," Martel goes on. "Considering the way you ran outta here last time, I said to myself, 'This shit must be *real* important if dude is willing to show his face around here again.'"

Jus flinches internally this time.

"So what's up, my man? I know you ain't come over here to stand in silence. What's this about?"

An easy(ish) in. "Uhh . . . Quan," Justyce says. Not real graceful, but it's out.

The way Martel's face goes all scrunched with confusion, however, makes Jus wanna suck it back in.

He forges ahead instead.

"He and I have been in communication for the past six months or so—"

"MY Vernell's been communicating with *you*?"

Oh boy.

"Yes, sir. I paid him a visit before returning to school back in January, and we've been communicating through letters ever since."

Now Martel's eyebrows lift and the corners of his mouth turn down. He looks almost . . . impressed? Which quickly morphs into suspicious. "The hell y'all been 'communicating' about?"

Now Jus has to tread carefully. He *knows* what he says next will either create a solid foundation for his outlandish request or give Martel every reason in the world to call the request outlandish. He kicks his shoulders up in a strategic shrug. "Really just trying to encourage him. One of my high school teachers took over as his educational coordinator, and he asked me to help Quan keep his head high." A lie, but a necessary one. "He got his high school diploma."

Martel lights up like the fireplace blazes Justyce got used to seeing all around New Haven in the wintertime. "Did he, now?"

"Mmmhmm."

"Well, do the damn thing then, Vernell!"

Justyce smiles. This is going better than he expected.

"That same teacher also got him a new lawyer," Justyce continues, jumping in with both feet. "There's a chance Quan—Vernell's—rights were violated the night of his arrest."

Martel's not smiling anymore. "Can't say I'd be surprised."

"Well, if they were, he could very easily be acquitted. Really, depending on the severity, the whole case could get thrown out—"

"I'm fully aware of how the legal system works, young buck."

Whoops.

"Well, that's why I'm here," Jus says. "The lawyer's working hard, and if Quan winds up getting to go free . . ."

"I'm listening."

(Has this dude not heard of context clues? Damn.)

"I guess, uhh . . . what I'm tryna say is . . ." *Deep breath, Jus.* "Umm . . . if he gets out . . . would you, uhh—"

215

"I'm not a fan of all the *uhh*s and *umm*s, young brutha. Say what you mean and mean what you say. Before I run out of patience."

Shit.

"Well, I'm here to ask: If he gets out, will you let him free too?"

"Let him free? What you think, I hold people hostage?"

Backtrack, backtrack. "No, no, that's not what I mean—"

"So what *do* you mean?"

Okay. Maybe a different angle . . . "I mean you no disrespect, sir—"

"Quit with the 'sir' shit, Justyce. Just get to the point. While you still got the chance."

MAYDAY, MAYDAY . . .

"Look, Quan's been working real hard. He's finally got a suppo—uhh, I mean a teacher who sees a lot of promise in him. He's got a case manager who actually cares and a counselor *really* helping him work through some stuff. And he's seeing a potential future for himself, which is something I don't think he had much of a vision for before."

A corner of Martel's mouth ticks up, and Jus wants to ask what he's smiling about, but he resists. "What I'm saying is he's able to see a different path now. He has no idea I'm here—would likely be *real* mad if he knew—but I truly believe he has a lot to offer the world, and with a little bit of help, he can pursue his dreams."

"And what dreams are those, Justyce?"

Damn!

"Well, I can't say specifically, but I know he wants to take care of his mom and sister and set a good example for his brother."

Martel doesn't respond this time.

"As I said before, I mean you no disrespect, Martel. And as *you* suggested, my coming here is a sign that I see this as life or death. I think we both know that if Quan gets out—*when* Quan gets out, cuz I really believe he will—he's gonna seek out the familiar. Then all of his hard work will've been for naught. So I'm asking you to NOT let him back in. With you. And your guys."

Martel's eyes narrow to slits and his head slooooowly tilts to one side.

So that's it then. Justyce is officially a dead man.

He *knows* his life is about to end when Martel looks him over head to toe and back again, then leans back in his rounded throne and crosses his arms. With a smirk. "You got a lotta damn nerve, boy."

There's no way Jus can hold the eye contact now. But he refuses to let his chin drop. Instead, he fixes his gaze on the poster of Huey Newton hanging over Martel's head. He learned all about dude in his History of the African American Experience course this past semester. *That* was a dude with "nerve"—

"What's in it for me?" Martel suddenly says.

Which certainly gets Justyce's attention. "Huh?"

"You come up in here with this outlandish-ass request . . . What do I get out of it?"

"Uhh—"

"There you go with the *uhh*s again, Justyce."

"I'm sorry, I'm sorry." Justyce gulps, looking everywhere *except* at Martel. Even though he knows he's gonna have to when he asks the next question.

So he does. "What . . . do you want?"

"That teacher."

"Huh?"

"The one who helped Vernell get his diploma. I want him here twice a week. Working with my boys so they can get their GEDs."

"Oh." Hope this doesn't backfire . . . "I'm sure he'd be cool with that."

"And Vernell can never come back here."

Jus doesn't know *what* to say to that.

"Ever. Matter fact, get his family outta here too. I don't wanna see none of them. Far as I'm concerned Vernell Banks doesn't exist. I see anything or anyone that suggests otherwise, we got a problem. Understood?"

"Yeah." *What the hell is Jus even agreeing to right now? Uproot and replant a whole* family?

"Lastly: his debt will have to be repaid. With interest. In a timely manner."

Jus wants to ask how a person who doesn't exist can owe a debt, but now doesn't seem like the time for jokes. "Heard."

"I'll have Trey contact you with those details. Understand that I'm holding *you* personally responsible. Something goes awry . . ."

Martel cuts Jus a look that lets him know he definitely, 100 percent does *not* want a single solitary thing to go awry.

"Responsibility accepted, sir—I mean . . ."

And Martel smiles. Warmly. "You a trip, man. Vernell is lucky. Most dudes around here don't get a friend like you. Keep it up."

"Oh. Thanks."

"Now get the hell outta my house."

Justyce doesn't have to be told twice. He tries to keep his cool as he heads back up the hallway to the exit, but he's pretty sure his heart has stopped beating.

As he pulls the front door open, he hears the words *keg stand* and sees the shoulders of three wildly different young men at the porch rail suddenly quake with laughter.

"You a straight fool, Jared," Trey says.

"Got *my* ass wanting to go to college . . ." from Brad.

And Justyce smiles. Because despite knowing that stepping out of Martel's house this time means stepping *into* way more than he bargained for, that there's still a life—*lives*—on the line, right here and right now, Justyce McAllister feels something he hasn't felt in a long time:

Free.

11

Debt

Quan hasn't been sleeping well, and he's about 96 percent sure Doc can tell.

Thing is, Doc is part of the problem. Technically, Quan's not even supposed to be meeting with Doc anymore: he graduated two months ago, so the court-mandated "education component" of his juvenile detainment is over.

Been over.

But somehow, Doc is still here. Still showing up twice a week and giving Quan assignments to complete. Apparently, everything he's doing now is aimed at earning college-level credits that'll be transferable once he's out. Attorney Friedman and Liberty talked to some people and did some stuff Quan didn't know was possible to set the whole thing up.

At Doc's request.

Doc, who also

mentioned some

grant he got that

will help him start

a tutoring service

that he eventually

wants Quan to work

for. Because Quan's

good at math.

I have a hunch you'll be able to expound *and make the numerical concepts relatable to the disenfranchised populations I intend to serve,* Quan can imagine Doc saying.

(Except he's not imagining it.)

(Doc really did just say that.)

"Quan . . . you falling asleep on me, man?"

A hand touches down on Quan's shoulder, and his drooping eyelids **SNAP** wide. "Huh?"

"You're getting drool all on your brand-new materials." Doc gestures to the open *Principles of Economics* textbook on the table in front of Quan.

And when Quan looks down at quite the saliva stain, what word leaps off the page at him?

DEBT.

(*Why the hell is there a* B *in it?* he thinks.

Is it for unnecessary burden? Bane *of his existence?*

Maybe it's there to remind him who's boss—)

"What's going on, man?" Doc startles Quan again. "You're drowsy. Unfocused. Bags under your eyes could carry my groceries."

Quan snorts.

"You're not sleeping well, I presume."

Now Quan looks away. Which, in this case, is its own answer.

"You been talking to Tay?"

About this *stuff? No.*

"Yeah."

Doc doesn't reply to Quan's reply, so Quan knows Doc's doing the laser-beam-eye mind-read thing. Where he stares at Quan all hard with his freaky green eyes all narrowed and reads—or so it feels—all Quan's thoughts and shit.

Quan *can't* look at Doc now because if he does . . . well, there's so much swirling around his head—a lot of it in the shape of dollar signs—there's a chance some of it will leak out the corners of his eyes in the shape of

wet drops.

And Quan can't have that, now can he?

He does wonder what Doc can see. The sleeplessness, sure. But can he also see the four prongs of fear, worry, help-lessness, and hopelessness propping the sleeplessness up?

Can he see the bizarre letter Quan received from Mama last week, telling him that she, Dasia, and Gabe were mov-ing out to the suburbs?

Or maybe he can see the conversation Quan had with Liberty where she let it slip that she turned down a job offer so she could stay on his case file.

Perhaps, though, he can see what's *really* been keeping Quan awake at night . . . because two days after the family relocation letter, Quan received an envelope that had one of Martel's drop houses—the one Trey used to stay (still stays?) in—as the return address.

And inside *that* envelope was something so eerily familiar, Quan dropped it as soon as he got it unfolded.

A ledger.

Using the template Quan created when he used to keep Tel's books.

Stuffed to the edges with delineated *dates* and *details* and *costs*.

All related to Quan's family.

There's

cash and
fuel fill-ups

groceries and
prescription meds

home services and
hot meals.

Any reference to *Dwight* is notably absent, a relief considering the twenty-two months Quan's been locked up on these charges. Good to know *that* debt is settled.

But still.

The ledger has a total.

What Quan owes a man who now wants nothing to do with him.

Because with that ledger came a one-word note:

Exactum.

It's the same one-word note that was delivered to Tel's clients when he no longer wanted to be in business with them. A command and threat in one: ***Pay up and disappear, or else.***

And while Quan was certainly shocked—and he'll admit, hurt—to receive one of Martel's famous "severance statements," what's really got his goat are the numbers.

His debt.

Because if he's in monetary debt to Tel, he's gotta be in *some* kinda debt to Tay.

He's definitely in debt to Attorney Friedman, so certainly also to Liberty.

Ain't no telling how much debt he's in to Doc.

And Justyce?

It'll be a miracle if he's able to look that guy in the eye (ever) again.

He hates it, but that damn ledger keeps shoving Quan's least-favorite questions right to the forefront of his consciousness:

WhyIsAnyoneHelpingHim? WhyDoesAnyoneCare? What AreTheyExpectingInReturn? How'sHeSupposedToPayAnyone Back? WhenWillTheReckoningCome?

Then the worst one of all:

H o w L o n g T i l l T h e y R e a l i z e H e ' s N o t W h o T h e y T h i n k H e I s?

Because he isn't.

He's no scholar or visionary or future leader of America.

He's a dumb kid who made a bunch of dumb decisions that have put him so deep in debt with EVERYONE, it feels like drowning.

Yeah, he loves his family more than life and is good with numbers. But that don't compute to "worthwhile investment of time, energy, and resources."

> *But flip the script, LaQuan,* he can hear Tay saying
> in his brain the way
> she did in his last session:
>> *If you were*
>>> *ME,*
>> *and I was*
>>> *YOU,*
>>> *would you invest in*
>>> *ME as YOU?*

"Yes," he said without thinking twice.

> *But why?*

"Because it's you. Obviously."

> (She rolled her eyes. A nonverbal *you're*
> *missing the point, LaQuan.*)
>> *What if it wasn't me? What if it was a kid*
>> *LIKE you?*
>> *One with your exact history?*

Quan had to think then. But not for long. Because that answer was obvious too. "I'd still invest."

Invest what?

"Time. Energy. Resources . . ." The next word shocked him as it popped off his tongue; it bounced around the room in an echo-ish way that the others hadn't: "Belief."

Belief?

"Yeah. Everyone should have *somebody* who believes in 'em. Like no matter what they've done. Somebody who won't give up on them."

Then:

"No strings attached."

He *did* get the point then. *HE* was willing to do for someone else what was being done for him. At no cost and with no strings. It was the right thing to do.

Period.

And yet . . .

"So you planning to tell me what's going on, or should we—"

Doc doesn't get the rest out because there's a BUZZZZZ and then the door to their classroom space *flies* open.

"MA'AM, you can't just barge in, there are PROTOCOLS for a reas—"

But that brown bowling-ball-headed bark gets cut off too.

"Jarius, LaQuan, I need you both to come with me," Attorney Friedman says with such authority, the air in the room would get in line if she told it to.

Quan and Doc look at each other, wide-eyed.

226

"Ma'am! I'm gonna hafta ask—"

"There's something you need to see," she continues, lifting a hand. (Quan's never seen his least-favorite guard's mouth shut so fast.)

"Right now."

Snapshot:

Two Boys,
an Attorney,
a Teacher,
and a Disgruntled Guard
in a Conference Room

Quan almost trips over his own feet when he follows Attorney Friedman through the open door of the Fulton Regional Youth Detention Center conference room and sees the likes of Justyce McAllister seated at the long table.

Justyce, who gives Quan a brief nod before facing back forward. And who's wearing a suit. Quan can tell Justyce is trying *real* hard to stay in Professional Negro mode—and he's sure Justyce knows how intensely Quan is roasting Jus in his head. But the fact that he's *here* expands the space around Quan just enough for him to breathe a little easier.

Still doesn't know what he's doing here, though. What *any* of them are doing here.

"Jarius, Quan, if you'll have a seat, please." Attorney Friedman has moved to the top of the room and leans over to say something to a guy at the head of the table with a laptop open.

And as soon as Quan's butt hits the chair, an image appears on a screen he didn't notice behind laptop dude. A screen that takes up half the wall.

Quan's eyes dart around and then shoot up to the projector, his mind kicking into scheming high gear as different ways of smashing the clunky white device to pieces, destroying it irreparably, spin through his head like a highlight reel.

Because on the giant screen is a grainy image of a sparse room with a table and two chairs.

And sitting in one of the chairs is Quan. With his hands cuffed behind him.

A sharp pain shoots through Quan's shoulder as the memories stampede into his head. He can feel his chest begin to tighten, so he shuts his eyes and does some deep breathing, knowing it's better for everyone to see this than one of his signature panic attacks. Takes himself away (mentally at least).

The feeling of warmth jolts him back into the room after who knows how long, and as Quan's eyes latch on to the contrast between his brown forearm and the pale hand resting there, a woman's voice speaks:

"You okay?"

More of the room comes into focus, and despite all the damn eyes on him right now, the thing Quan is most aware of is his "high-risk/violent" orange jumpsuit compared to the other clothes around him. The *normal* clothes (though Jus in a suit is a little outta the ordinary).

Man, what he wouldn't give to wear normal clothes again. Jeans. Cotton shirts that aren't rough and scratchy. Jordans instead of the standard-issue Jesus-style flip-flops.

In the image on the screen, Quan can see the upper third of a white hoodie that he knows has the Champion logo printed on the front in red and blue. A little ironic considering where he's sitting, but still: it was his favorite hoodie.

And he misses it.

So damn bad.

"I'm good, Ms. Adrienne," he says to Attorney Friedman, who is kneeling beside him in her nice suit. "Just caught me off guard, is all."

Her hand moves from Quan's arm to her own forehead. "I am so sorry. I wasn't thinking. I should've warned you—"

"It's cool, it's cool," Quan says. He glances at Justyce, who nods as his brown thumb appears just above the lip of the table. "I'm good. For real." Pretty much to the room. "We can keep going."

Attorney Friedman bobs her head once and rises to her high-heel-clad feet to click her way back to the front of the room.

"Thank you all for being here," she says, popping right back into lawyer mode. "As both Justyce—who has seen it—and Quan here are aware, the footage you're about to watch was captured the night of Quan's arrest almost two years ago. An intern at my law office was kind enough to condense the nineteen-plus hours' worth of tape into the twelve or so minutes you're about to see."

She presses Play, and Quan watches, rapt, as a dude that both is and isn't him morphs, over the course of three visits to the small room where he was questioned, from a young man with resolve to a little boy who just wants to be left alone. Round one, he sat tall, his shoulders pulled back, but by the time they shoved him into the chair for round three, Quan was done: he immediately slumped down and put his forehead on the table.

Quan knows the whole thing's been "condensed," as Attorney Friedman said, but it still blows him away how quickly they were able to break him down. Especially considering how long he's been up in *here*—and how long he could be in actual *prison* if this case goes forward and he's convicted.

Just as quickly as the video starts, it's over.

Twelve minutes of footage.

Anywhere between a decade and *life* locked away.

So why is Justyce grinning like somebody just slid him a platter with all his wildest dreams on it?

"I was right, dawg!" Jus says, his suited persona slipping. "Based on that story you told me, I had a hunch—"

"What are you talkin' about, man?" Cuz Quan's getting mad now. (Though seeing Justyce's face morph makes Quan wish he could take it back.)

"Were you not watching the tape? Your Miranda rights were clearly violated, Quan."

Now Quan's the one whose face is morphing. "Huh?"

"LaQuan, every time you stepped into that room, you invoked your right to remain silent," Attorney Friedman says. "Literally. And the questioning officers bulldozed right through that. Considering how much time elapsed between the first and final questioning, I also suspect coercion—"

"Coercion?"

"Were you given food?"

"No."

"Water?"

"No."

"Allowed to sleep?"

"No."

"Permitted to use the restroom?"

"No . . ."

She smiles. Which seems inappropriate, but Quan gets it. "Coercion," he says.

She nods. Just once. "Correct."

Justyce jumps back in: "But even without the coercion, your confession would be inadmissible—"

"*Should* be inadmissible," Attorney Friedman says. "I've filed a motion to suppress it."

"Considering the look on the DA's face when he called us in to get the tapes, though?" Justyce winks at Quan.

"Justyce," Attorney Friedman says with a warning edge, but she's also fighting a smile.

Quan looks around the room, trying to take it all in. "So what . . . does this mean? Exactly?"

"Well, sounds to me," Doc chimes in, his voice cutting through Quan's confusion like a sword through butter, "like one step closer to freedom, Mr. Banks."

July 23

Dear Quan,

Look, don't tell anybody (hopefully they don't open this letter before giving it to you), but a document from the state lab was delivered to Mrs. F's—Attorney Friedman's, my bad—office this morning that I think you might find real interesting. I've included a photocopy. She's probably gonna be mad at me when she realizes I opened mail while she was out, but when I saw that the return address on the envelope was the DA's office, I couldn't resist.

Anyway.

As the document shows, you were right: the ballistics don't match. Two bullets were pulled from Castillo's body, and neither matches the caliber of the pistol found with your prints on it.

I believed you, obviously, but this proof should help to advance our case. I'm sure you've been at least a little nervous since entering that not-guilty plea, so I thought maybe this would offer you some comfort.

Attorney Friedman's been hounding the judge to set a trial date. I think you made a good call, going with the bench trial—not having to select a jury should make things go faster. At this point, the state has no concrete evidence and zero eyewitnesses, so unless the prosecution has a trick or two up its sleeve that we don't know about, there's no way they have enough to convict you. We expect to hear back on that motion re: the confession any day now, and once the court rules to suppress it—deciding not to would be a flagrant miscarriage of justice—the state will have nothing to go on.

Hopefully you'll be outta there soon.

Keep your head up, all right, dawg? We're almost there.

My girl says "Hi!" by the way. She's sitting right here and wants me to tell you she can't wait to meet you.

More soon.

You have my word.

Sincerely, your friend,
Justyce

One Month Later

August 27

Dear Justyce,

I feel kinda wack writing to you already—it's only been two days since you left—but I'm struggling today. Liberty came to tell me she's also headed back to school, and even though hers is local, the end of her internship means the end of her being on my case. Shit sucks.

On top of that, I found out this morning that they're cutting my lessons with Doc to once every other week. Something about budget changes and labor laws.

Also sucks.

I dunno, man. Trying not to be all dramatic, but knowing I'm not gonna see three of you who were keeping me afloat makes me feel like I'm going under. Still no word on that motion to suppress the confession, and still no court date.

I'm tryna keep my head up like you told me to the last time you visited with Attorney Friedman. (I'm clearly a changed man cuz that poke you gave me in my damn forehead woulda gotten you punched in the past.) But it's hard.

With each day that passes, it's getting harder.

I did talk to my moms the other day, though. She told me

my sister's hair is starting to grow back. So that's a relief.
I knew her little feisty ass wouldn't let that shit beat her.

Sure wish she could come dump some of that optimism on me.

Hope you made it back to school safe.

Write back soon?

Sincerely,

Quan

12

Done

For the past five nights, Quan's been having wild-ass night-mares. From being hauled from his cell, dragged down a dark hallway, and tossed into a pit full of the bones of dead black boys, to watching Tomás Castillo crawl out his grave and chase Quan to Martel's house, where all of his boys are wait-ing to shoot him dead.

Tonight's involved a white-eyed Justyce in a three-piece suit opening Quan's chest and frowning at whatever he saw inside before summoning Doc to come take Quan out with a shotgun. And for the fifth night in a row, his eyes have popped wide in his cell, but he's been unable to take a breath.

Or move.

All started on his second anniversary in this place. Seventy-nine days after entering a not-guilty plea.

Which means he's been in jail for seven hundred and thirty-five days.

He can feel sweat at his hairline and along his neck. And he can't breathe.

But something's different this time.

> *I don't know what's going on with him. Eyes are open, but he ain't respondin'. Look like he seen a ghost . . . Do I need to get the medic?*

"Excuse me."

> *Ma'am, you're not permitted inside the cell—*

"Quan?"

Quan knows that voice.

He just wishes he could respond to it.

> *Ma'am, your presence inside the cell is a violation of protocol—*

"Sir, this young man is in distress, which I think is a fairly top-notch reason to suspend your *protocol* for a few minutes," the female voice says. "Quan? It's Tay. I'm here, all right?" She puts a hand on his forearm. "The paralysis will subside shortly, and I'll be here."

But what is she doing here?

"Is everything okay, Octavia?" Another familiar female voice.

"Yeah, he's all right," Tay replies. "Just needs a minute for his system to relax. Guessing he had a nightmare."

> *And now they're **both** breaking protocol,* the male voice laments.

"We'll be outta your hair shortly, sir," says the second woman.

"Figuratively speaking . . . ," Tay mumbles. (So it's Bowling Ball giving them a hard time. Of course.) "We appreciate your patience," she says loud and clear.

"Appreciate my patience." Tuh . . .

"Can he see or hear us?" the second woman's voice continues.

"Hear, most likely. See, not quite sure. Sleep paralysis can be tricky. His eyes haven't moved, so I'm guessing he's not truly seeing much of anything," from Tay.

"That's gotta be terrifying."

"Certainly wouldn't call it fun," Tay replies. "Okay, he's coming down. Saw his thumb move—"

All at once, the vise releases from around Quan's chest, and two faces blur into view, one brown with a (fresh) blond fade, and one white with a dark-brown shoulder-length bob thing. He takes the breath that saves his life (or so it feels) and shuts his eyes.

Opens them again to make sure he's not still dreaming.

The women are still there.

"Well, this is embarrassing," he says.

Tay and Attorney Friedman both laugh.

"What day is it?" Quan says, confused. He meets with Tay on Thursdays and Attorney Friedman every other Monday. He's pretty sure today is neither.

"Wednesday," Tay says. "Sit up. We have something to tell you—"

The young man is awake now. I need you to vacate the cell. Protocol.

"Lord have mercy, Jesus," Tay says under her breath. It makes Quan smile. Even though, yes: her and Attorney Friedman being *in* his cell is . . . weird. And a little uncomfortable. It's not exactly tidy in here. Though better for there to be books scattered all over the place than something else, he guesses.

Also: he's in his boxers.

As soon as they've exited and are out of view, Quan snatches his jumpsuit from where it's plopped in a heap of wrinkly tangerine fabric on the concrete floor and pulls it over his drawers and tank top. Socks on with *utmost celerity*, as he learned from Doc, then his feet are in his sandals.

Part of him wants to slow down. If Tay *and* Attorney Friedman are here, something happened.

And it's potentially something bad.

Because why else would

his lawyer

AND

his counselor

be necessary?

Too late, though. He's already crossed the threshold into the cellblock common area.

And they're waiting for him.

No one says a word as they stroll up the hall toward the

line of little meeting rooms. Quan eyes everyone carefully, Bowling Ball and the superintendent included, trying to catch the vibe, but comes up empty because *he's* too nervous. Sweat trickles down his side from his armpit, and he gulps.

Then they're in a room and he's sitting. The guard is leaving and the door is closing.

Quan is still breathing.

Barely.

Nobody's saying anything.

But then . . .

Attorney Friedman is smiling.

And looking at Tay.

Who is smiling too.

"So," Attorney Friedman says. "We have some news."

"A lot of it," says Tay. "And it's likely to be overwhelming."

"Which is why Tay is here," from Attorney Friedman. "If at any point you need me to repeat something, say so. And if you need me to stop so you can process, I will."

"Deal?" asks Tay.

(Quan's not really feelin' this *tag-team* thing
    they got going on, but whatever.)

"Deal," he says.

Attorney Friedman: First off, good morning!

Tay: Really, Adrienne?

Attorney Friedman: What?

246

Tay: Let's not give the young man a heart attack.

Quan: Please.

Attorney Friedman: My apologies. Just seemed rude not to say it.

Quan: [*Takes a deep breath.*] Good morning.

Attorney Friedman: So, we heard back on our motion.

Quan: [. . . *Stops breathing.*]

Attorney Friedman: Thrilled to report that the court ruled to suppress your confession on account of the flagrant Miranda violation as well as suspected coercion.

Quan: [*Breathing—and beaming—now.*] You're serious?

Attorney Friedman: Oh, there's more. Also heard back on my request for an expedited trial date.

Quan: [*Stops smiling.*] Okay . . .

Attorney Friedman: The trial is going to be . . .

Quan: [*Bated silence.*]

Tay: Rude, Adrienne.

Attorney Friedman: Sorry, sorry. Never.

Quan: Huh?

Attorney Friedman: Got a call from the DA himself yesterday afternoon. State's dropping all charges.

Quan: [*No longer breathing . . . again.*]

Attorney Friedman: DA said with a suppressed confession, no murder weapon, and no witnesses, they don't have much of a case. You're getting out of here, LaQuan.

Quan: [*Still not breathing.*]

Tay: Quan? You okay?

Quan: [*Turning to her.*] Is she saying what I think she's saying?

Tay: [*Smiling.*] I do believe she is.

Attorney Friedman: I definitely am.

Quan: [*Looking back at Attorney Friedman.*] So . . . I'm done?

Attorney Friedman: Yep.

Tay: You're done.

Attorney Friedman: Totally done.

He's done.

Six Months Later

Snapshot:

Two Young Men
on a New (to Them)
Playground

The two BIG boys—if you can even call them that—chillin'
at the top of the climbing wall are wildly oblivious to the
glares aimed at them from the *actual* children below.

Who want to climb.

"Justyce, you realize we look like grade-A creepers, right?"

"Man, whatever. We're chaperoning your brother's party.
What better lookout point is there than the highest spot in
the park?"

Quan shakes his head.

And smiles.

"I still can't believe you're *here*. It's your spring break, man.
You 'sposed to be on a beach somewhere, checkin' out honey
bunnies from behind the darkest sunglasses you can find."

"Now *that* is some creeper shit, dawg."

Quan laughs.

"Real talk, though, that whole *broke college student* stereo-
type is legit," Justyce continues.

"Whoa now, man. You can't be calling yourself *broke*
around me if we're gonna be friends. That shit's a mind-set.
And it's contagious."

Justyce snorts. "You sound like Martel."

Which makes Quan's heart pinch. And he bets Justyce
can tell because his boy doesn't say anything else.

"You seen him recently?" Quan asks even though he shouldn't.

Justyce nods. "Yeah. Went over there to help DeMarcus with an essay Doc assigned him as soon as I got in. Even took Jared's wack ass with me. You'd think he and Brad were long-lost brothers the way them fools be actin'." He shakes his head.

Quan sighs and looks off into the distance. Not too long after he got out, Justyce—aka Earth's Worst Secret Keeper Ever—broke down and told him the bizarre-ass story behind the *Exactum* notice he got from Martel. Including the part where he volunteered Doc's instructional services to the members of Martel's organization.

Doc, Justyce told him, took the whole thing in stride considering the stakes. But Doc made it clear to Justyce that Jus *would* be working for the tutoring service Doc founded and planned to expand. Without pay.

Quan, though, *does* get paid. And paid well. *Way* better than he feels he deserves, but that's another thing he's learning. From Doc, not Martel: *Don't undervalue yourself by undervaluing your skill set.*

Doc also made Quan open up a checking account on his eighteenth birthday and taught him how to use checks even though the practice is basically obsolete. (Doc isn't hip to instant money-transfer apps.) And Quan is still mailing a check to Martel's home address every couple weeks to cover his debt—though oddly enough, not a single one has been cashed.

"So they're all doing well?" Quan asks without looking at Justyce.

"Yeah, man. They are. Still . . . doing business. The way they were before. But learning and growing too. Your boy Trey recently found out he's gonna be a dad."

"Wait, for real?" What the hell did Martel have to say about *that*? Quan wonders.

"Yep. Apparently he and this young lady have been dating for a while? I think her name is Trinity. You know her?"

An image pops into Quan's head of Trey hugging up on a gorgeous brown-skinned girl on one of those *before* nights when everything was different. He smiles. "I do."

"Dawg, I been knowing Trey most of my life, and I ain't *never* seen that guy as happy as he was when he told me the news yesterday."

Now Quan's eyes drop to his knees. Man, what *he* wouldn't give to see Montrey Filly happy. Much as that dude been through. "That's amazing, man. Give him my congratulations."

When Justyce doesn't respond, Quan looks up to find the guy *examining* him the way Tay does sometimes. Quan shoves Justyce's shoulder. "Bruh, why you eyein' me like that? You tryna fight?"

"Man, whatever." Justyce shoves back. "Let's talk about

something else since I can tell your ass is gettin' all nostalgic and shit."

"Quit cussin'. There's babies in the vicinity."

Justyce waves him off. "So how are you, dawg? Everything copacetic?"

"Who are you, Doc?"

"Just answer the damn question, you question-dodger."

Quan sighs. And smiles again. Truth be told, it's nice to have Justyce around even temporarily. Dude is genuinely the best *friend* friend Quan's ever had. "Things are solid, man. Took a minute to get into the new swing once I moved back in with my moms—the suburbs are weird as fu—"

"Language."

Quan laughs. "It's weird out here is what I'm saying. Like mad *quiet*. No streetlights. And stuff, this park included, closes at like seven p.m." He shakes his head. "I definitely had way more freedom—and way fewer chores—during my months at the Drays', but I can't really complain."

Right after his release, Quan moved in with Doc and his husband to spend a little time getting reacclimated before going back home. And it turned out to be a good thing: he really struggled at first, and having not one but *two* successful black men around to support and guide him was mad helpful. Even seeing two dudes crazy in love—something that was admittedly uncomfortable for Quan at first—was helpful: when he met Liberty for lunch to shoot his shot . . .

and she shot him right down by letting him know she had a girlfriend, Quan hadn't batted an eye.

"You and SJ good?" he asks Justyce now that he's got love on the brain.

"Ah, we're taking a break," Jus replies.

"Wait, *what*?!"

Justyce grins. "I'm just playin'. We're great, man. She's in Israel right now on her Birthright trip."

"You better hope she don't meet some bangin' Jewish dude with more money than you, Mr. Broke."

"Whatever, dawg. I know you heard the phrase *Once you go black . . .*"

Quan laughs so hard he almost falls off the rock wall. "Between me and you, I wish I could find me a woman like Liberty."

"Wait, did I tell you about how Jared randomly saw her and her girl at a restaurant, and his idiot ass tried to holler at her and got curved so hard, he *had* to get a crick in his neck?"

Now Quan's laughing even harder. "You're not serious, man."

"Oh, I am. Dude is dumb as a rock sometimes. Those oblivious entitled-dude roots creep up and choke his *good* brain cells from time to time," Jus continues.

"You can take the rich white boy out the country club . . ."

"But you can't take the country club out the rich white boy. I feel it, man."

The boys—young men, really—lapse into a steady silence.

Which is the only reason they can finally hear the angry jeers from the fourth and fifth graders beneath them. "You fellas mind coming down so we can, you know, *climb?*" comes the voice of a brown kid with slick black hair. Sunhil, Quan believes little dude's name is.

"Yo, who you think you talkin' to like that, huh?" Quan says.

Sunhil's eyes go wide. "I'm sorry! I didn't mean—"

"I'm just messin' with you, kid. Come on, Justyce."

The two climb down and stand to the side, watching as pairs of kids, Quan's brother Gabe included, race each other to the top.

"Can you believe my baby brother is *eleven*, man?" Quan says, crossing his arms as he watches the long-limbed, superhero-loving kid he spends just about every Saturday with get bested in a climbing race by a tiny redheaded freck-led girl who moves like a damn spider. "That's two years older than when *we* met. Shit's crazy."

"Yo, you remember the rocket ship?"

Quan turns to look at Justyce like he just asked if blue whales can fly. "Are you really asking me that? Of *course* I remember the rocket ship. It was my favorite mode of imagi-nary travel, thank you very damn much."

Justyce drifts off to somewhere Quan can't go, and his eyes narrow. "You miss it?"

At first, Quan doesn't respond. Because he really has to

think about it. His eyes roam the always-clean park space. Touch on his mom, laughing with Sunhil's; his sister, all boo'd up on the swings with some li'l boy Quan definitely wants to punch; his brother, sitting at the top of the climbing wall with his arms raised in triumph on his birthday; his best friend right beside him.

Only thing missing is his dad. But they write to each other weekly, and Quan's been out to visit the old man a couple times, so even that's okay.

He smiles. "You know what, man? I don't."

"You don't?"

"Nah," Quan says. "No need to go to outer space."

Justyce smiles, and Quan knows Jus knows exactly what he's going to say next.

So he does: "Everything I need is right here."

(Consider this one indefinite, and therefore un-date-able)

Dear Justyce,
    Thank you.
    For everything.

                    Sincerely,
                    Vernell LaQuan Banks Jr.

Author's Note

This is the hardest book I've ever written. From the research to the content to the painful pieces of my own past I found myself unintentionally mining, Quan's story took more out of me than I knew possible to pour into a piece of "fiction."

I put fiction in quotes because despite this being the *most* fictionalized book I've done thus far, it felt the most *non-fictional* as I was working on it. In truth, I know more Quans than I know Justyces. More boys—and girls—doing their best to just stay *out* of trouble in a world that seems bent on shoving them into it. Kids, mostly poor, African American, and living in less than ideal circumstances (euphemistically speaking), who experience their first suspension from school and are said to have "behavioral problems" before they reach double digits in age. Classic school-to-prison pipeline. Look that up.

I spent time in juvenile detention facilities interacting with the kids who are being held there, and hearing their tales of downward slide. Many of them had stories like Quan's: an incarcerated parent, deeply traumatic home lives, and limited resources for survival, let alone situational improvement. Most of the decisions they made—especially the ones that landed them in detention—were rooted in desperation: A seventeen-year-old who joined a gang after his dad left and his mom slowly unraveled; he got tangled up in drug use to numb the hurt he didn't know how to deal with, and eventually committed a gang-related murder. A fifteen-year-old who was being bullied and eventually got fed up and shot the bully in the head. A kid whose parents would boost him through the windows of houses so he could let them in for the robbery. And the one who keeps winding up back in detention because she takes her ankle monitor off whenever she gets out and is placed on house arrest.

Many of the kids I've met *know* they're going to be locked up for a long time. *Most* of the girls have been sexually abused or trafficked (and they are *all* under eighteen). I've met a couple of boys who have pregnant girlfriends awaiting their release.

All this to say: the stuff in this book is very real.

I did take a few fictional liberties. For instance, Justyce likely wouldn't have been able to visit Quan in the facility. In the state of Georgia, visitation is limited to immediate family, significant others, and attorneys. Were he truly incarcerated here in Georgia, he would've been permitted to send two postcards per week unless his family provided additional stamps. It is also unlikely (unfortunately) that Quan would have such a solid team of people—friend, caseworker, therapist, teacher, and attorney—rallying around him.

Which was the hardest thing of all about telling this story: knowing the most fictional part is the support Quan receives.

But I think we can change that, dear reader. No matter how young or old you are, we all have the power to positively impact the people around us *before* they get to the point Quan did. Sometimes all it takes to bring about a shift in direction is knowing there's *someone* out there who believes you're valuable. That you have something positive to offer the world.

If you're a reader who *hasn't* had a person like that in your life—someone who looks at you and sees good things—please, please, please know that *I* do. I don't have to meet you to know that you are infinitely valuable and that you have something no one else on earth has to offer the world. Because you are the only you.

If you're a person fortunate enough to have people who believe in you, pay it forward. The majority of the people you interact with are fighting some kind of battle. Sometimes a smile or a genuine "Hey, how are you?" has the power to move an emotional mountain. A listening ear can make a day, and an "I believe in you" could completely change a trajectory.

Anyway. I'll stop there.

Thank you for reading, and please don't forget: you *are* wildly important and have a lot to offer no matter how you feel. Resist when the world tries to convince you otherwise.

Acknowledgments

As usual, there are more people who should be thanked than I'm gonna be able to name, but know that if you contributed to this book in ANY way—early readers, encouragers, *Dear Martin* fans who demanded a sequel (this is admittedly maybe *not* what you had in mind, but still), authenticity checkers, etc.—I appreciate you.

Specifics: Phoebe—for telling me you wanted a Quan book and letting me write it the way I wanted to. Barbara—for being cool with this thing Phoebe wanted me to do. Danny and Zay—for texting me that one day and asking me to tell *your* story . . . letting me know that you were looking to *me* to amplify *your* voices by writing about a dude whose experiences mirror yours more than Justyce's did.

Nigel—thank you for your continued willingness to create the space and time for me to live out these massive and ever-evolving dreams of mine. Jakaylia and Rodrea—for reading this thing mad early and letting me know if you were moved or not. Jeff, Megan, and Sarah—for being a part of #TeamAttorney, reading this early, and checking my legal stuff. And #TeamRandomHouse: y'all are lit. Special shout to Kathy and Kristin, who texted me while reading to tell me you were reading—and enjoying.

And most of all, I want to thank YOU, dear reader (especially if you're actually reading these acknowledgments). You being at this point in the book hopefully means you read through the novel itself, and for that, I am eternally grateful. Boys like Quan don't get a lot of positive attention, so you giving him yours—even though he's fictional—means a lot to me.

May you take everything you gained from this book and put it toward improving this wild world we live in.

Catch up on Nic Stone's spellbinding debut— a #1 *New York Times* bestseller!

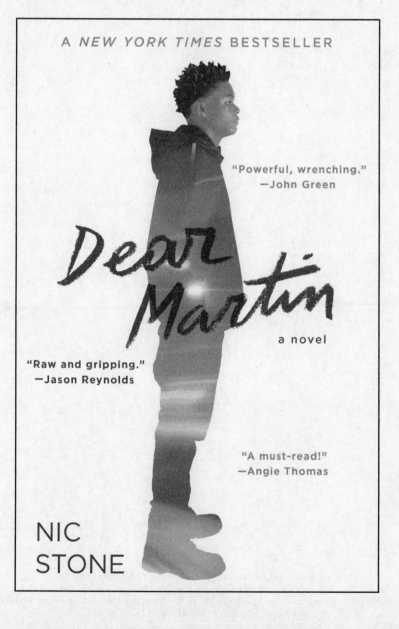

A *NEW YORK TIMES* BESTSELLER

"Powerful, wrenching."
—John Green

"Raw and gripping."
—Jason Reynolds

a novel

"A must-read!"
—Angie Thomas

NIC
STONE

CHAPTER 1

From where he's standing across the street, Justyce can see her: Melo Taylor, ex-girlfriend, slumped over beside her Benz on the damp concrete of the FarmFresh parking lot. She's missing a shoe, and the contents of her purse are scattered around her like the guts of a pulled party popper. He knows she's stone drunk, but this is too much, even for her.

Jus shakes his head, remembering the judgment all over his best friend Manny's face as he left Manny's house not fifteen minutes ago.

The WALK symbol appears.

As he approaches, she opens her eyes, and he waves and pulls his earbuds out just in time to hear her say, "What the hell are you doing here?"

Justyce asks himself the same question as he watches her try—and fail—to shift to her knees. She falls over sideways and hits her face against the car door.

He drops down and reaches for her cheek—which is as

red as the candy-apple paint job. "Damn, Melo, are you okay?"

She pushes his hand away. "What do you care?"

Stung, Justyce takes a deep breath. He cares a lot. Obviously. If he didn't, he wouldn't've walked a mile from Manny's house at three in the morning (Manny's of the opinion that Melo's "the worst thing that ever happened" to Jus, so of course he refused to give his boy a ride). All to keep his drunken disaster of an ex from driving.

He should walk away right now, Justyce should.

But he doesn't.

"Jessa called me," he tells her.

"That skank—"

"Don't be like that, babe. She only called me because she cares about you."

Jessa had planned to take Melo home herself, but Mel threatened to call the cops and say she'd been kidnapped if Jessa didn't drop her at her car.

Melo can be a little dramatic when she's drunk.

"I'm totally unfollowing her," she says (case in point). "In life *and* online. Nosy bitch."

Justyce shakes his head again. "I just came to make sure you get home okay." That's when it hits Justyce that while he might succeed in getting Melo home, he has no idea how he'll get back. He closes his eyes as Manny's words ring through his head: *This Captain Save-A-Ho thing is gonna get you in trouble, dawg.*

He looks Melo over. She's now sitting with her head leaned back against the car door, half-asleep, mouth open.

He sighs. Even drunk, Jus can't deny Melo's the finest girl he's ever laid eyes—not to mention *hands*—on.

She starts to tilt, and Justyce catches her by the shoulders to keep her from falling. She startles, looking at him wide-eyed, and Jus can see everything about her that initially caught his attention. Melo's dad is this Hall of Fame NFL linebacker (biiiiig black dude), but her mom is from Norway. She got Mrs. Taylor's milky Norwegian complexion, wavy hair the color of honey, and amazing green eyes that are kind of purple around the edge, but she has really full lips, a small waist, crazy curvy hips, and probably the nicest butt Jus has ever seen in his life.

That's part of his problem: he gets too tripped up by how beautiful she is. He never would've dreamed a girl as fine as her would be into *him*.

Now he's got the urge to kiss her even though her eyes are red and her hair's a mess and she smells like vodka and cigarettes and weed. But when he goes to push her hair out of her face, she shoves his hand away again. "Don't touch me, Justyce."

She starts shifting her stuff around on the ground—lipstick, Kleenex, tampons, one of those circular thingies with the makeup in one half and a mirror in the other, a flask. "Ugh, where are my keeeeeeeys?"

Justyce spots them in front of the back tire and snatches them up. "You're not driving, Melo."

"Give 'em." She swipes for the keys but falls into his arms instead. Justyce props her against the car again and gathers the rest of her stuff to put it back in her bag—

which is large enough to hold a week's worth of groceries (what is it with girls and purses the size of duffel bags?). He unlocks the car, tosses the bag on the floor of the backseat, and tries to get Melo up off the ground.

Then everything goes really wrong, really fast.

First, she throws up all over the hoodie Jus is wearing.

Which belongs to Manny. Who specifically said, "Don't come back here with throw-up on my hoodie."

Perfect.

Jus takes off the sweatshirt and tosses it in the backseat.

When he tries to pick Melo up again, she slaps him. Hard. "Leave me *alone*, Justyce," she says.

"I can't do that, Mel. There's no way you'll make it home if you try to drive yourself."

He tries to lift her by the armpits and she spits in his face.

He considers walking away again. He could call her parents, stick her keys in his pocket, and bounce. Oak Ridge is probably *the* safest neighborhood in Atlanta. She'd be fine for the twenty-five minutes it would take Mr. Taylor to get here.

But he can't. Despite Manny's assertion that Melo needs to "suffer some consequences for once," leaving her here all vulnerable doesn't seem like the right thing to do. So he picks her up and tosses her over his shoulder.

Melo responds in her usual delicate fashion: she screams and beats him on the back with her fists.

Justyce struggles to get the back door open and is lowering her into the car when he hears the *WHOOOOP* of a short siren and sees the blue lights. In the few seconds it takes the police car to screech to a stop behind him, Justyce settles Melo into the backseat.

Now she's gone catatonic.

Justyce can hear the approaching footsteps, but he stays focused on getting Melo strapped in. He wants it to be *clear* to the cop that she wasn't gonna drive so she won't be in even worse trouble.

Before he can get his head out of the car, he feels a tug on his shirt and is yanked backward. His head smacks the doorframe just before a hand clamps down on the back of his neck. His upper body slams onto the trunk with so much force, he bites the inside of his cheek, and his mouth fills with blood.

Jus swallows, head spinning, unable to get his bearings. The sting of cold metal around his wrists pulls him back to reality.

Handcuffs.

It hits him: Melo's drunk beyond belief in the backseat of a car she fully intended to drive, yet *Jus* is the one in handcuffs.

The cop shoves him to the ground beside the police cruiser as he asks if Justyce understands his rights. Justyce doesn't remember hearing any rights, but his ears *had* been ringing from the two blows to the head, so maybe he missed them. He swallows more blood.

"Officer, this is a big misundersta—" he starts to say, but he doesn't get to finish because the officer hits him in the face.

"Don't you say shit to me, you son of a bitch. I knew your punk ass was up to no good when I saw you walking down the road with that goddamn hood on."

So the hood was a bad idea. Earbuds too. Probably would've noticed he was being trailed without them. "But, Officer, I—"

"You keep your mouth *shut*." The cop squats and gets right in Justyce's face. "I know your kind: punks like you wander the streets of nice neighborhoods searching for prey. Just couldn't resist the pretty white girl who'd locked her keys in her car, could ya?"

Except that doesn't even make sense. If Mel had locked the keys in the car, Jus wouldn't have been able to get her inside it, would he? Justyce finds the officer's nameplate; CASTILLO, it reads, though the guy looks like a regular white dude. Mama told him how to handle this type of situation, though he must admit he never expected to actually need the advice: *Be respectful; keep the anger in check; make sure the police can see your hands* (though that's impossible right now). "Officer Castillo, I mean you no disresp—"

"I told your punk ass to shut the fuck up!"

He wishes he could see Melo. Get her to tell this cop the truth. But the dude is blocking his view.

"Now, if you know what's good for you, you won't move or speak. Resistance will only land you in deeper shit. Got it?"

Cigarette breath and flecks of spit hit Justyce's face as the cop speaks, but Justyce fixes his gaze on the glowing green *F* of the FarmFresh sign.

"Look at me when I'm talking to you, boy." He grabs Justyce's chin. "I asked you a question."

Justyce swallows. Meets the cold blue of Officer Castillo's eyes. Clears his throat.

"Yes sir," he says. "I got it."

RAW, RIVETING, AND UNDENIABLY REAL.

Catch up on every Nic Stone novel!

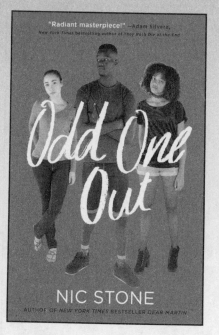

Underlined

A Community of Book Nerds & Aspiring Writers!

READ

Get book recommendations, reading lists, YA news

DISCOVER

Take quizzes, watch videos, shop merch, win prizes

CREATE

Write your own stories, enter contests, get inspired

SHARE

Connect with fellow Book Nerds and authors!

GetUnderlined.com • @GetUnderlined

Want a chance to be featured? Use #GetUnderlined on social!